THE MARQUESS AND I

Forever Yours Series

STACY REID

THE MARQUESS AND I is a work of fiction. While reference might be made to actual historical events or existing locations, the names, characters, places, and incidents are either the product of the author's imagination or are used fictitiously, and any resemblance to actual persons, living or dead, business establishments, events, or locales is entirely coincidental.

THE MARQUESS AND I

Edited by AuthorsDesigns

Cover design and formatting by AuthorsDesigns

Dusean, always and forever.

FREE OFFER

SIGN UP TO MY NEWSLETTER TO CLAIM YOUR
FREE BOOK!

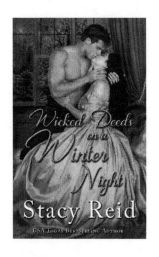

To claim your FREE copy of Wicked Deeds on a Winter Night, a delightful and sensual romp to indulge in your reading addiction, please click here.

Once you've signed up, you'll_be among the first to hear about my new releases, read excerpts you won't find anywhere else, and patriciate in subscriber's only giveaways and contest. I send out on dits once a month and on super special occasion I might send twice, and please know you can unsubscribe whenever we no longer zing.

Happy reading!
Stacy Reid

that I look for when reading romance and deserving of a 5-star review. "—*Isha C., Hopeless Romantic*

"Wicked in His Arms—Once again Stacy Reid has left me spellbound by her beautifully spun story of romance between two wildly different people."—*Meghan L., LadywithaQuill.com*

"Wicked in His Arms—I truly adored this story and while it's very hard to quantify, this book has the hallmarks of the great historical romance novels I have read!"—*KiltsandSwords.com*

"One for the ladies...**Sins of a Duke** is nothing short of a romance lover's blessing!"—*WTF Are You Reading*

"THE ROYAL CONQUEST is raw, gritty and powerful, and yet, quite unexpectedly, it is also charming and endearing."—*The Romance Reviews*

An Unconventional Affair

Mischief and Mistletoe

A Rogue in the Making

The Kincaids

Taming Elijah

Tempting Bethany

Lawless: Noah Kincaid

Rebellious Desires series

Duchess by Day, Mistress by Night

The Earl in my Bed

Wedded by Scandal Series

Accidentally Compromising the Duke

Wicked in His Arms

How to Marry a Marquess

When the Earl Met His Match

Scandalous House of Calydon Series

The Duke's Shotgun Wedding

The Irresistible Miss Peppiwell

Sins of a Duke

The Royal Conquest

The Amagarians

Eternal Darkness

Eternal Flames

Eternal Damnation

Eternal Phoenyx

Single Titles

Letters to Emily

Wicked Deeds on a Winter Night

The Scandalous Diary of Lily Layton

CHAPTER 1

London, Midsummer night.

"Sweet merciful heaven," Alasdair Hugh Morley, the Marquess of Westcliffe muttered hoarsely.

An enchantress.

Nothing else made sense for how she commanded his attention. The fickle beauty stood perfectly motionless, her head tilted left, the graceful and delicate arch of her neck on tantalizing display, a sensual smile on her lips. Lady Willow Rosalind Arlington, daughter of the Duke and Duchess of Milton, was exceptionally beautiful, though not in the way society would deem fashionable. Some like his mother would say the young lady was too plump, her hair too dark, and her skin too pale, but to Alasdair, she was a rare ruby in the midst of glittering diamonds.

The sight of her filled him with an unwelcomed rush of pleasure. Lady Willow was indeed a vision. Her alabaster skin was a vivid contrast against the high waisted sapphire colored gown she wore. Her dark hair was piled high on top of her head with flowers woven between the strands, and though her body was plump, she was sweetly curved. He had realistically known she would be in attendance at tonight's Midsummer ball and thought he had been prepared. But nothing in his wildest imagination could have readied him for the emotions she evoked after all these years—a bewildering mix of joy, cold rage, and heated desire.

Devil take it.

Her lips curved deeper into a mysterious smile, tempting, rousing his memory of their succulent taste. What the hell was wrong with him? Had he not learned his most painful lesson at her hands? Words he would never be able to forget slithered to the forefront of his mind, the last place he wanted them to be.

I am to marry His Grace, the Duke of Salop. My father accepted his offer yesterday. I thank you for the kind attentions you bestowed on me, but I cannot marry you.

Please forget my earlier declarations. I should not have been so bold as to say I love you and will marry you. You are the third son, Alasdair...my father will never accept your courtship.

Words that had been said almost six years ago still had the power to torment him, and here he had thought he was ready to see her, that she was only a phantom of his past. If only she had known then his chances of inheriting the title would be greater than anyone imagined. After all, he was now the Marquess of Westcliffe and the last of his cursed line.

He almost forgot all the pertinent reasons he was present at the Duke and Duchess of Milton's annual Midsummer Night's Ball. Alasdair despised balls and social gatherings, finding them tedious and unimportant. His mother had never understood his position. She had been aghast that he had not been amenable to attending tonight's event, which had turned into a celebration of the Duke of Wellington's victory.

While he was glad they were now safe from the advancement of Napoleon's troops and machinations, Alasdair had only to close his eyes, and the carnage of war swam across his vision. There had been no victor. Hopes and dreams had been crushed, and the lives of thousands of men, women, and children had been obliterated.

He glanced around the brightly lit ball, the extravagant decorations, and the crush of people as they jostled to greet each other, their facile chatter ringing in his ears over the rousing strains of the orchestra. Women and men swirled across the ballroom, laughing and talking, glittering in their fineries, thrilled to be at the most coveted event of the season, soaking in the gaiety and music. How oblivious they were to the atrocities of life. And suddenly he was glad, for they were fortunate to be ensconced in such a bubble, away from fear, pain, despair, hunger, and terror.

Though he now faced a situation almost as daunting as being on the battlefield. His purpose tonight was calculated, though it left a bitter taste in his mouth. Finding a wife, a young heiress. Any heiress would do, though he hoped to select someone from the marriage mart with a modicum of intelligence and a pleasant countenance. While he did not yearn for love, he would speak with and gaze upon his marchioness for years to come, and he would like to hold her in more esteem than what she brought to his pockets.

"The young lady you are staring at so avidly,

and quite rudely, is Lady Willow, His Grace's only daughter. I am sure you are acquainted with her from your visits to Hadley House years go," his mother, the Dowager Marchioness whispered almost conspiratorially. "Lady Willow has not made an appearance in London in years, and the family is very tightlipped as to the reason. Her dowry is rumored to be twenty-five thousand with an annuity of ten thousand pounds. Let us greet our hostess and seek a reintroduction to her daughter. I am sure the waltz will be danced tonight. You should secure her for your partner."

He grunted noncommittally. The last place he wanted to be was near Lady Willow. Touching her, smelling her. Seeing those beautiful moss green eyes turn to distaste, and he hungering for a simple smile from her. His thoughts made him cold, and the rage he had buried burned just a bit brighter. Maybe he needed to fulfill the promise he had made to himself years ago. The promise to seduce the bewitching beauty and soothe the tormenting hunger he had for her and then walk away. Satisfaction filled him at the thought. Was she promised to a gentleman? He hoped not, for while he still wanted to punish her with pain and pleasure, he did not dally with women already spoken for.

His mother glanced up sharply at his lack of response. "You promised, Alasdair," she admonished with a frown.

"Hold your tongue, Mother." He placed her hand on his arm and strolled with her through the throng toward the card rooms, never taking his eyes from Lady Willow. "You wheedled and prodded, and I am in attendance. I will select my dance partners without nudges from you."

Her hand tightened on his arm, and he glanced down. Fire snapped in gray eyes almost identical to his own, and her lips closed in a flat line of irritation. But he would not be swayed. He was already doing his duty, and she had harangued him every day on what she considered was expected. He knew very well her agenda tonight was to help him select a potential bride, for his mother spent the majority of her days worrying about his marital status.

"If you are not eager to be reacquainted with Lady Willow, you should then make your introductions to Lady Madalene, the eldest daughter of the Earl of Gilmanton. Rumor has it he has doubled her dowry."

Without answering, Alasdair deposited his mother in the card room and excused himself from her presence. He understood her urging, but the only young lady currently engaging his attention was Lady Willow.

Unable to stop the desire, his gaze automatically sought for her. The yearning on her face drove the air from his lungs. It was intense, painful, hauntingly lovely, and suddenly he wanted to be the one to give her whatever she craved. Foolish to be certain, for he was not a man to give into flights of fancy or romantic idiocy. Not after she had shattered his heart, not after the atrocities of the war.

He followed the line of her gaze and frowned. She looked toward the potted plants by the terrace. Hardly a thing to inspire the wistfulness on her lovely features. She moved as if pulled by a greater power toward the music. Her steps were hesitant, halting, as if she were unsure of what to do. Teeth sank into a pouting bottom lip, and she worried at it before changing the direction of her steps.

Her sudden turn had her colliding into the footman with the tray of champagne.

The crash was jarring. She went white, and one of her hands fluttered to her throat. She glanced around as if looking for someone, and if he was not mistaken, she paled even further at the silence generated by her accident. A swell of murmuring rose, and a few ladies even craned their necks to observe the mishap, no doubt eager for some gossip to impart tomorrow, even if it was mundane. Why did she not walk away? Instead, she gripped the folds of her gown, panic chasing over her features. Her throat convulsed on a swallow, and vulnerability settled on her face.

Alasdair was disturbed by the wave of tenderness that swept through him. He gritted his teeth in annoyance. Tender affections were the last emotion he wanted to feel for her. Where was the rage that should incite him, to want to cause her harm after her callous disregard? He searched for it and came up blank, startling him, given the number of bitter thoughts he'd had about her over the years after she had rejected him. *Not good.* The only thought he should spare Lady Willow was in seducing her, taking everything he had been denied because of her inconsistency, branding her body and soul with the taste and feel of him so that when he turned from her, she understood the depth of pain he had felt at her refusal. But the panic on her face tugged at the cold place inside of him, and he wanted to reassure her and soothe whatever caused her to display such anxiety.

He strolled toward her casually, ignoring the murmured greetings and the nods from other men.

Don't do it you fool. Walk away…Ignore her distress.

Yet his feet continued. He was drawn by a greater need than simply to see her reaction when she realized he was now the Marquess of Westcliffe, and that he had every intention of exacting the false promises she had made. Everything in him demanded to see her lovely face up close, to see the smile that had once had the power to render him senseless, to drown himself in the beauty of her green eyes, and to hear her voice…sweet, yet husky, with the ability to jerk his cock to life from a mere chuckle.

He was a damn fool.

CHAPTER 2

Mortification threatened to drown her. Lady Willow could still hear the shocked murmurs and whispers at her blunder. How could she have allowed herself to relax so?

"How clumsy!" a voice twittered.

She knew the rules, understood the expectations, and she had failed. On the one night to prove she was more than capable, she'd let her family down. The desire to flee overwhelmed her, but she remained frozen. Where would she go? Though the darkness was a familiar place, panic rose swamping her senses.

Where was her companion, Lady Olivia? Willow had promised her grandmother, the

Dowager Countess of Montrose, she would be circumspect in everything she did tonight.

You must not accept any offers to dance. Nor must you partake in any of the refreshments. You will stand close by me and give no indication of your situation.

The impervious voice of her grandmother still rang in Willow's ear, and panic clawed at her throat. This was it. The independence she had been fighting for over the last year would take a severe blow. There would be no more outings, and the picnic at Hampstead Heath she had been hoping to attend with Olivia would be banned. Willow's family's over-protectiveness would stifle any joy she had left.

"Why is she just standing there?" a curious voice demanded.

The crush pressed in on Willow, and she felt suffocated. Her mind drew maps of the house, and she planned her path of escape. If memory served, she was standing near the third terrace window, and she only had to step three paces, turn left and walk about twenty paces forward to escape into the closest garden. From there she could make her way to the inner alcove.

She stepped forward and almost screamed when she bumped into someone.

"Blasted hell!" a man cursed. "There's champagne all over my waistcoat."

She pressed her hands to her stomach, hoping to stop the twisting nerves writhing inside. Willow tilted her head toward the voice. "Forgive me, I did not see you there."

The muttered curse that slipped from him had a blush climbing her cheeks. Certainly, he thought she would not have heard over the dreadful noise of a packed ball.

Olivia, where are you? Willow screamed in her mind, trapped in a sick sense of uncertainty and fear. It had been years since she had allowed herself to be with so much of Society. Surely Olivia should be back from the retiring room? Willow's friend and companion had only disappeared for a few minutes with a promise to return shortly.

Had her grandmother or her parents noticed her mishap?

The murmurings got louder, her skin became clammier, and Willow parted her lips to ask for assistance. A thing she was loathed to do, but it couldn't be helped, the last thing she wanted to do was embarrass her parents, the hosts of tonight's extravagant ball.

A fleeting touch at her elbow froze her. A scent

of midnight moss and wild rain filled her nostrils. The smell was unique, subtle, compelling, and different from the mess of oranges, jasmines, and lavender that crowded her senses.

Familiar…

"Steady." The voice was low, soothing, and confident. "I believe the next dance is promised to me."

As if he had only been waiting for such a hint, the waltz was announced, and a ripple of excitement traveled through the crowded assembly. The dance was shockingly scandalous, and from all the gossip Olivia had shared with Willow, many wondered if the Duchess of Milton would order it to be played tonight. Willow's pulse hammered as firm hands pulled her closer. She could not allow this, though a part of her rebelled in protest at her foolish hesitancy. Since Olivia had tried to teach Willow the beautiful and intricate steps, she had always secretly yearned to waltz, but with a partner who understood her circumstances.

"My lord, I…" Her throat closed, and she frowned. Was he a lord? But then who would display such boldness and be so inappropriate as to command her to the ballroom floor, without so much as an introduction? She should only be grateful for his assistance, but his impropriety had a startling effect. More than gratefulness suffused her. Excitement slithered through her, quick and startling, and it was because of this unexpected intrusion in her very mundane, predictable, and lonely life. She tilted her head and offered a grateful smile. "I am Lady Willow, I thank you for your timely intervention. My slight mishap was generating much unwanted attentions."

"Lord Westcliffe at your service, my lady," he murmured somewhat caustically.

Westcliffe?

Willow's heart pounded in her chest, and she lifted her eyes to where she hoped his were. "I thank you for your kind offer, but I do not wish to dance. If you escorted me to the drawing room, I would be grateful. I feel as if I am fit to swoon in this crush." She lifted her hand, and he guided it to rest on his arm.

There was a beat of silence, and she fancied she could feel the curiosity that roiled from him. *Oh no.* She prayed it was not someone she should recognize, though she knew who the title belonged to, Alasdair's eldest brother, Marcus. But he had died from the fever if her recollection was correct. Secluded so far away from town and the fashionable season, she could only rely on news from Olivia to keep abreast with the ins and outs of the *ton*. And there her knowledge was sorely lacking.

"Would you honor me with a turn in the gardens instead?"

"A turn in the gardens?"

"Yes. The moon is full, the stars are bright, and the terrace windows are open so we won't miss any of the beautiful music."

She was not chaperoned, but she did not care. Olivia was not needed to take a simple turn in the gardens. "I would appreciate a breath of fresh air, my lord."

The thrill of even being asked for a stroll was overwhelming, and Willow did nothing to pause her steps as she weaved through the crush with him leading the way. From his movements, she could feel that he made his way to the far-left sash windows. There they would move to the outer terrace, and there were steps that could lead them to an alcove.

Cool night air washed over her skin. They were on the balcony. She knew how many steps to traverse the pathways to the gardens to lead into the alcove, and she followed him, not objecting to his highly inappropriate behavior. She matched the rhythm of his stroll, still silently counting as they navigated down the steps. She was inexcusably reckless following him, even if he had rescued her, even if she had wanted to be away from the crush of the ball. She inhaled to steady her anxiety and was once again buffeted by a hint of something disturbingly familiar. Breathing deeply of this elusive scent, she felt a jolting response...a familiar one that only he had been able to rouse in her.

She stumbled to a halt, jerking her fingers from his clasp. "What is it?"

It couldn't be. The voice of this man was deeper, rasping against her nerve endings with potent sensuality. "Alasdair?"

"Lady Willow," he drawled with an icy bite.

Good heavens. "How...I..."

Had it been a jest when he introduced himself as Lord Westcliffe? Had he been mocking her? She forced herself to stop the frantic churn of her thoughts.

"For a moment I thought you had not recognized me, Lady Willow."

Without the noise of the ball, everything sharpened into painful comprehension. A gentle caress against her cheek had anticipation shivering low in her stomach. Had he touched one of her tendrils? "Of course I recognized you," she said huskily.

"I recall how fleeting I truly was in your life, hardly someone worth remembering. It seems I was mistaken." His voice was laced with soft menace.

She stepped back a pace. Hardly worth remembering? She had dreamed of him at the crest of each dawn and nightfall for years. Memories of past kisses, shared dreams, and nightmares rushed through her, causing her heart to tremble in both fear and joy.

Then relief crashed into her. He was alive! Her older brother Quinton had marched to war, and she knew Alasdair had bought a commission as well. No matter how she had hinted, then outright asked her brother of Alasdair's well-being, she had been met with tightlipped silence. Happiness gathered in a sweet ache in her chest. *Alasdair*. But he had introduced himself as Lord Westcliffe. Bewilderment churned inside, but she struggled to show an unaffected mien. She could only pray she succeeded with the depth of emotions twisting through her, confusing in its intensity. Horror clashed with joy; shame burned with delight. It took enormous will to just keep breathing.

"I knew you to be more loquacious. I never thought it was possible to render you speechless."

She liked the cadence of his speech, the deep sensual wash of his voice. It was hardly a thing to notice against the coldness of his tone. "I—" The reality of being so close to him, speaking with him, after years of yearning for the impossible made her lightheaded.

She swayed.

His hands gripped her, warm, strong, and the pleasure of his touch burned her. She drew back, startled, and slammed her hip into a wrought iron table. A hiss slipped from her lips, and she thrust her hand backward gripping the table to steady herself. He was suddenly there, hands lightly circling her waist, supporting her.

"Are you hurt?"

Though her side throbbed, she shook her head, trusting he would see her clearly from the dozens of torches she knew lit the stone balcony and the inner alcoves.

"Are you truly the Marquess of Westcliffe?" she managed to ask.

She felt the tension that sifted through his frame.

"Answer me," he urged. "Are you hurt?" She tried not to read too much in his concern.

"No. Are you truly the Marquess of Westcliffe?"

"Yes." His voice held a hint of pain and darkness.

She shifted in his embrace and grasped for his arm. He clutched at her, and she slid her fingers through his. "I am deeply sorry for your losses. I cannot imagine the torment your family has endured." He had been a third son. What had happened for him to now hold the title?

His grip tightened briefly on her fingers before releasing her. Then he stepped away.

She instantly felt bereft of his warmth. "Thank you for whisking me away. For a moment, I thought I was about to swoon. My brothers would never let me forget if I had behaved so delicately," she said softly, ignoring what she really wanted to say.

The questions jumbled inside her, and she had to grit her teeth to prevent them from spilling out. Why had he not returned? Where had he been? Did he have an attachment? She wanted to know everything that had happened in his life for the past six years. It was very silly of her to have such a desire. He had left without looking back...not once.

If he had, he would have known how much she had needed him.

"You were never a lady to indulge in histrionics. Why were you so affected?"

She gave an unladylike shrug. "I have found that the attention of Society can be intimidating."

"Enlighten me."

Willow paused, annoyed with her slip. Society's perceptions of her inferior circumstances were the last thing she wanted to discuss. "I have not seen you, we have not seen or spoken to each other in six years, Alasdair." Her throat tightened so the words begging to tumble from her lips could not escape.

"And?"

I missed you. Yet the words would not come. It would be utterly foolish to reveal her affection after the disregard he had shown her. She should return to the crush of the ball and escape to her room. To be alone with him was highly improper. Society would not care they had been close friends, and he would certainly be livid if he was forced to marry a young lady in her circumstances. Though knowing all of this, she was compelled to continue their conversation, to hear his voice, the cultured yet roughened tone, and possibly once again hear that soft chuckle of pleasure whenever he was amused or delighted.

Oh, if she could only make out his features. He seemed so chillingly uncivil, very different from the laughing young man she had known. How much had he changed? What was he now like? At one and twenty he had been striking. She clearly remembered his swarthy masculine beauty. Eyes that were the gray color of a winter storm, the slant of his cheekbones, the sensual curve to his lips, and dark golden hair that he normally wore in a messy way. His frame had been lean and hard from his many outdoor activities. Did he possess that same arrogant tilt of his head when he spoke?

Confound it.

The need to touch him, to learn his face, arose hot and thick inside her. It was this desire that allowed her to regain her senses. "I must return inside. Will you escort me, Lord Westcliffe?"

She knew the placement of every piece of furniture, the location of every window and door and every inch of grounds of Hadley House; yet tonight's ball had disconcerted her. Nothing was as it should be. Even the scents that normally guided her were overpowered by the flowers that decorated the ballroom.

"I have missed you as well, Willow."

She froze.

"You have learned nothing of hiding your emotions. I can see the desire and questions," he admitted softly, a curious undertone of fascination and something darker evident in his voice. "I would be a veritable liar if I did not admit to missing you."

She struggled to understand the dip in his voice, the intent that saturated his words. *Intimate*. Though his words were innocuous, they rasped with intimacy. But beyond the intimacy there was anger, and it scraped along her nerve endings.

"You are angry," she said blandly. It made no sense for her to pretend.

His soft chuckle was mirthless. "Why are you not married, Lady Willow? Your Duke Salop, was he not all you dreamed of? Could it be he found out behind your beauty lay a heart as cold as the winter?"

She flinched but looked to the direction of his voice. "I will not rehash the past with you, Lord Westcliffe. We were both young and foolish…and this is now."

Footsteps crunched on gravel as he moved closer. *Too close*. His heat seemed to reach out and caress against her skin.

"I was young and acted like an imbecile, Lady Willow, you were a fickle and unfeeling bitch."

She gasped at his crudeness, and a wave of sadness rolled through her because underneath his anger she heard the pain. She closed her eyes for she understood, even after all these years, she still hurt whenever she thought of the times they had spent together. The hopes and love that beat inside of her for him. It had caused her torment, to know he had been driven away without knowing the depth of affection she held for him. It had been expected that she would snare a duke. Third sons, no matter how charming, gallant, and handsome had been forbidden to her.

"This may not mean much to you now, but I loved you, Alasdair. My family told me you were not suitable. I was almost persuaded not to love you, and I never got the opportunity to express my regret. My father fought against the idea I wanted to be your wife, and I caved in to his demands because of fear."

"Almost persuaded?"

She could hear the derision in his voice and wondered if his lips twisted in that way they normally did when he was disgusted. Unable to help herself she reached forward, and her fingers bumped his chin.

He froze.

The need to make him understand burned inside of her. She had longed for such an opportunity for years, never really believing she would see him again. "Yes, almost. I regretted my harsh words, I regretted conceding to my father, and I tried...I tried to visit your home because I—"

"Liar," he breathed softly against her lips, and her heart jerked. She had not felt him move.

"Alasdair, I—"

"No," he growled, placing his hands on her hips. "Sweet lies once again spill from your lips, and I am a damnable fool because I want to believe you cared enough to travel to Westerham Park. The only thing I am interested in is to claim what you denied me, denied *us*."

Shock made her stiffen, and anger surged in her veins. "I was young, but I loved you with every breath in me. I drove you away with foolish words because I feared my father would destroy you if I did not relinquish the idea of us. But if you loved me as ardently as you professed, why did you not try to persuade me to run away with you to Gretna

Green? You left," she whispered in outrage. "I denied us nothing."

He jerked her to him, and disconcerting sensations rushed through her. She was acutely aware of him, his size, his hardness, and most of all his scent.

"Unhand me, my lord."

"Never will you refer to me as lord," he drawled with an icy bite. "I will only hear Alasdair from your lips when I take what I have long dreamed of."

"I beg your pardon?" she whispered furiously and pushed at his chest.

He released her, and her anger spiraled because she wished for the strength of his embrace to return to her body.

"I want you to understand my intentions, Lady Willow. I will be exorcising you from my thoughts. It has been six years, and I still dream of your smile and laughter, of your taste, of your kisses and gentle opinion. No more. I will make you want me until it is an unrelenting ache, and then I will bury my cock deep inside you. You will sob my name and claw my back, begging for the sweetest of pleasure never to end, I will brand your soul with me, and when I am finished, I hope you will regret, as I do, the loss of us."

Utter shock had her hand fluttering to her throat. Then startling hope rose, pushing aside all other emotions. Was this not what she wished for every day? To feel passion, to taste it, to indulge in it? To be daring and independent of Society's derision and her family's overprotectiveness. But not like this...not with anger and pain, the voice in her heart whispered.

She stepped in closer to his warmth. "I am intrigued by this method you would use to make me beg, to make me ache so relentlessly." The words slipped from her before she thought of the consequences of being so bold.

He became so motionless, she fretted she had said the wrong thing. Then her ears picked up the hitch in his throat, the softly shuddered breath. She affected him just as he did her, despite the anger. The realization filled her with delight, and for the first time in years, Willow felt wicked... and wonderful.

A touch. A whisper of air passed over her lips, and she knew he had dipped closer than what was considered proper. A fleeting caress. She savored it, though their lips barely touched. Another breath puffed across her cheek. Every touch, whisper was a torment. But such a sweet torment. His scent flooded her senses, and acting on instinct, she rose on her toes and leaned forward. The taste of his lips was like spiced wine and strawberries. He stilled, and blood roared in her ears. She had kissed him! How shockingly improper and scandalous of her. She parted her lips to his entreaty. A soft groan slipped from him, then his tongue stroked the edge of her teeth. Not once did he draw her closer or press his body against hers. But she felt the heat of him, tasted the strength of him, and lost a bit of herself that she had sworn to keep protected, after enduring what had seemed like an endless nightmare.

His tongue glided over her lips and into her mouth. Though he had never touched her with such boldness, she reveled in his embrace. For once she pulled from this forbidden and exhilarating encounter, she would never allow herself to be in his presence again. How could she? While his promise filled her with scandalous temptations, she would not lead herself into more heartache. Not with this man.

A shiver cascaded down her spine. She itched to thrust her fingers through his hair, but she did not want to shatter the moment. Their kissing without touching seemed more intimate than if they had been grasping each other. She fixated on the taste and texture of his lips, learning and enjoying him. His lips were rough, hard and possessive. Instead of frightening her, Willow leaned more into his tantalizing warmth. Something hot and confusing unfurled inside of her. It created a throb that started from her breasts, down to her navel and even lower to her most intimate valley. His touch coaxed, tempted, and teased. Unable to resist, she ran a single finger against the hard length of his jaw.

He pulled his lips from her, breathing raggedly, and she sucked in an unsteady gulp of air when he nipped at her neck.

"Sweet," he murmured roughly. "You taste sweet."

She traced his brows, his nose, learning him, appreciating him. She sank her fingers into the length of his hair, her fingertips gliding through the thick yet silky strands, and she noted his locks were shorn much closer to his scalp.

Removing her fingers, she asked, "What are we doing, Alasdair?" Her voice came out husky, shaky, and heat climbed her cheeks at the undisguised need in her tone. But she needed to understand what they were really thinking. It was inconceivable that after meeting each other for the first time in years, they were doing this, whatever this was.

He kissed her lips tenderly, then whispered against her throat, "I do not know. This was not my intention tonight. Far from it, but you are temptation incarnate, so damn beautiful."

Willow's breath hitched. Beautiful? Did he not see her scars? Her thoughts derailed as he claimed her lips again. A moan slipped from her, and she swayed closer. She was losing herself, drowning in his scent and taste, needing him, and fear curled through her.

She would never allow herself to need another again.

Willow drew back from the warmth of him, overwhelmed by the pleasure elicited from only a kiss. "My lord, I—"

His hands cupped her cheeks. "I need to know. Is this why you kiss me with such passion, Lady Willow, passion you have never shown me before?" He touched his lips to the corner of her mouth. "Because I am now a marquess... not so low and insignificant to kiss, to touch?" he whispered, but the soft contempt in his tone flayed her.

No, she could not do this, not with so much pain between them. Her body railed at her for rejecting something she had long hungered for and never thought she would experience. But if she hurt so much now, what would she feel when he was through with her body and heart? She pulled from him, shifting left, and her hip slammed into another table, or was it a chair? A moan of pain slipped from her. Devil take it!

"You need to be more careful," he said. "Here let me help—"

"No! Please, I need a moment without your touch." Not caring what her admission revealed, she reached out and felt for the chair. Cold iron brushed against her skin. Grasping the back of the chair, she moved toward it and stubbed her toe.

"Bloody hell," the unladylike curse slipped from her in frustration.

"Are you always this accident prone?" He asked, soft amusement evident in his tone.

"Forgive my clumsiness," she said through gritted teeth.

"It is I who should beg your forgiveness. It was not my intent to disparage you. The lights from the terrace and gardens do not provide much illumination."

His footsteps shifted and moved from behind her to stop at her side.

"May I be of assistance?"

Tell him. She was being a coward, yet the words stuck in her throat. She wanted his escort to the library. They would never make such a journey without at least a few bumps and stumbles. The added tables and chairs and the crush of people were confusing. "I cannot see. I am blinded," she confessed thickly.

"I beg your pardon?"

"You heard me," she said softly.

A cool breeze nipped at her. Willow waited, feeling awkward and exposed.

"Blind?" his voice was neutral, all emotions buried.

She could feel the heat of his gaze as it roamed over her features, no doubt looking deep into her eyes. Did he notice the scarring at her temple? "Yes."

There was a swift intake of breath and then dreadful silence.

"I suspect you wish to take your leave, my lord. I only ask that you escort me safely to my grandmother. I will not hold you accountable for wanting to end our tryst."

"Our tryst?"

Her cheeks burned. That was how she had indeed been romanticizing their encounter. Foolish.

He slipped his fingers over hers, linking their hands together. "Willow, I—"

She pulled from him and straightened her spine. "No, Lord Westcliffe." She thought he flinched at her formality, but she pressed on. "I think we both needed tonight to happen. I am glad we spoke. While your offer to exorcise me from your dreams was indeed tempting, I fear I must decline. I propose you will have to find another method. I can feel the need in you to know what happened, but this is private for me, and it is not something I will share. Please do not press me, but I would appreciate you escorting me to the library, my lord."

She waited, her heart a drum in her chest.

"It will be my pleasure to escort you, Lady Willow," he said, lifting her hand to his arm.

His response hurt her when it shouldn't have. What had she expected? For him to deny her charge, to fight to have an affair? Very silly of her to be sure. After all, years ago when he had professed to adore her, he had walked away without looking back. Why would he fight now, when her circumstances were so inferior?

Foolish, foolish girl.

CHAPTER 3

Alasdair stood by the windows in the parlor, deep in thought. He had taken a morning tour of his main estate, Westerham Park, just on the outskirts of London, very near to Hadley House. The repairs were daunting, the park wall alone ran for almost five miles, and in many places, the stone needed to be rebuilt. Many tenant houses and cottages were in desperate need of fixing. Yet his mind invariably shifted to Willow.

Now he understood the shock in her voice when she had recognized him. The relief and triumph he had felt when he led her away from the ballroom was unwarranted. She had not been following and placing her trust with him, but with a faceless stranger. Willow was a woman he had banished from his thoughts years ago. All of his resolve should not have toppled from a mere glance. He'd rushed to her rescue without giving another gentleman a chance to intervene. The years had fallen away as memories of her laughter, and her joy in the simple pleasures in life had curled through Alasdair.

Now instead of feeling the justifiable anger of the callous way she had disregarded their love, all he felt was the unfulfilled ache of desiring her and sorrow. The surge of cold rage and the need to use her body had vanished. Why? A soft breath expelled from him, and he closed his eyes.

It was because of her blindness. The shock of her words had been a brutal punch to his system, and all thoughts of hurting her had vanished. The pain and vulnerability on her face had been deep; he would be an arse to even want to add to her suffering. Moonlight had spilled over her features, a shimmery glow, and her beautiful green eyes had stared at him sightlessly, her expression a fierce mix of resignation and pride. The pain of her loss still scythed through him. He had seen men ravaged with agony and grief over the loss of eyes and limbs in the war. He could imagine how she must have railed and cried. And he had not known. How long had she been without sight?

Upon his return home from last night's ball, it had been the first time he had slept without nightmares of war, or of his dying brothers. Instead, he had dreamed of her. Of how lonely and proud she had looked when she had confessed her blindness.

"I am very sorry for your loss, Willow," he had said as he discreetly returned her to the main house.

Inadequate words and silence had lingered between them. He had also dreamed of her kisses, of what it would be like to sink himself into her wet heat and hear words of love once again spilling from her mouth. It had been a mistake to touch her. Even now, the memory of her soft skin, so supple and smooth, sent a rush of need through his body.

The entire time he had walked toward the main house, he had berated himself for being foolish. He had let his anger cloud his judgement and the control he exercised over his emotions and actions. From a simple taste of her, everything in him had clamored to draw her deeper into the hidden alcove and take her. The knowledge she would be willing, had only served to make the lust burning through his body for her flare hotter.

He should move on from Willow and direct his thoughts to wooing an heiress, but it was damned difficult to do. He needed to know what happened to her. Why had Quinton not said anything to him? Alasdair had seen her brother just last week in Bath.

The drawing room door opened, and a cloud of perfumed lavender travelled inside. There was a rustle of movements as his mother settled herself. "I am thinking of taking a position with the Foreign Office," he said without turning around, contented to watch his sisters running through the maze in the garden without an ounce of decorum. A position in the Foreign Office was an offer Lord Liverpool had made Alasdair several months ago before he had inherited the title. He believed the offer would still be valid as the Prime Minister had admired his war efforts.

The only sound his mother made was a swift indrawn breath of, undoubtedly, outrage. He shifted, and with a glance at her face, Alasdair deduced it might very well be disgust. He smiled, though it was without humor. "Mother…"

She gripped the quill and pushed aside the parchment she had been composing her morning correspondence on. "You will not shame this family. A marquess does not work. You will not work. To even think to take such a position is to ruin your sisters when they depend on you… you will make them common," she spluttered.

Common? He swallowed the shout of laughter. She was absurd. "Filling a position at the Foreign Office will not make us common. We are on the brink of financial ruin, madam. I think that is the only ruin we should be worrying about."

After the death of his father several years ago, his eldest brother Marcus had assumed the mantle of leadership. He had been groomed for it, and he had made a good marquess. He had been loved and admired by many in Parliament, and in society. He had not been the marquess for long before influenza had claimed his life. Then Alasdair's next brother Charles, the spare, had inherited. While Alasdair had been fighting on the Peninsula, Charles had been living a dissipated lifestyle, one filled with wild debauchery, which had depleted their already modest financial situation. He had been unlucky enough to kill himself in a racing carriage accident right in Mayfair. Too warped in his own pleasures to adequately care for their estate, including their mother and their younger sisters, some would say it was a blessing he had been taken early.

Then it all had fallen to Alasdair—the mistake.

He had refused to consider what his two younger sisters were to his parents if, as the third child, he had been the mistake. He only knew he had to provide for them, settle them suitably in life, ensure their happiness, and protect their future. And he would do this at any cost. Annabelle was the eldest at eighteen, and Elizabeth was sixteen. He would have to put off Annabelle's coming out for at least another year, and she was already late. His mother would have the vapors if she knew he had leased the house at Cavendish Square.

"You will need to prepare yourself to get acquainted with the intricacies of Parliament. You are now Lord Westcliffe. Find yourself a wealthy bride and assume the mantle you were born for. Procure an heir and secure the title. You are the last of the Westcliffe line. As far as we know, there is no cousin to inherit. Do what is expected of you, Alasdair."

He raised a brow. The mantle he was born for? The question of succession was a thing that plagued his mother. He would admit that understanding he was the last of his line was disquieting, but he was still not moved to do all in his power to secure an heir. To provide for his siblings and his mother was to him of greater concern.

"My dear friend the Countess of Masheley mentioned to me very discreetly that you were seen leaving the gardens last night with a young lady."

He was careful to keep his expression schooled. From the curious look his mother gave him and the calculating gleam in her eyes, she could only refer to Lady Willow.

"I met many young ladies last night," he responded noncommittally.

Her head bobbed. "Yes, but only one you went into the gardens with."

At his silence, she huffed an impatient sigh. "Lady Willow comes from an extremely prominent and wealthy family. Her father is a duke, and her grandmother is a formidable Dowager Countess. Lady Willow has an ample dowry and political connections to help you take your place in this new fabric of society. Her circumstances should also make her eager for your attentions."

"Her circumstances?" he snapped, irritated with his mother. Lady Willow's lack of sight did not define her.

His mother shrugged indelicately. "Lady Willow is blind, and by all accounts, her parents have been hiding her away at Hadley House. From what I gleaned, she has not even had a season. They will be grateful for you to wed her."

No season and no wedding. The last time he saw her, she was supposed to leave for London with her mother to purchase her wedding trousseau for her marriage to the Duke of Salop. Could it have been that long? Was that why she was unwed?

"Have you discovered how she came to be blind?" Asking the question revealed too much of Alasdair's interest, but his gut burned to know.

"No. But that is irrelevant. It only matters her parents will be happy for your attentions and should have no objection to your suit. Lady Willow herself will be grateful. After the nuptials, she could stay in the country, so she is not an embarrassment."

Hot anger curled through him. "An embarrassment?" he bit out coldly.

His mother at least had the grace to blush. "I did not mean to be so callous. I sympathize with her plight."

It would be appallingly easy to decide to woo a lady for her money if it would help restore his family. If it would help to provide for his sisters when they would desire a season and a dowry. But could he marry a woman like Lady Willow for such a purpose? *Never.* She dreamed. He saw it... felt it, he had even tasted it. She yearned for love and passion, to be swept away in the enchanted realm of lust and love. Though he had burned to be inside her last night, it would be a sin to marry her unless he could offer her that.

Alasdair no longer believed in love and the dreams they had once shared, and he wouldn't succumb to such emotions again. He wanted a simple marriage with none of the emotions and none of the expectations beyond an heir and simple affection. That he would willingly give his wife. Affection, respect, loyalty. But never would he open himself to the hunger, the desperation of loving and needing someone, as he had done with Willow. And if what he heard last night was true, she was no longer an heiress, making her doubly unsuitable.

His lack of fortune was damning. He was responsible for the livelihood of hundreds of people. He had to do all in his power to remain solvent. But Alasdair had hope. He had sold much of the antique silverware, and the unique set of Meissen the family had been so proud of, to invest in a shipping venture. It would bring spices and silks. To improve their fortunes, he had also been gambling, a vice he had sworn to stay away from, after it had destroyed his father, and started the financial ruin they were on. But Alasdair had been winning, and he was careful. He had won twenty acres of prime London property in a game of hazard a few nights ago. He had thought to divest himself of it for quick gains but hesitated. He would pursue every avenue to develop it for profit, regardless of such ventures being viewed as beneath a marquess. Despite what his mother believed, he would not leave only one option open to salvage his family.

"I see you are not aware of the rumors surrounding Lady Willow's name."

Predictably, his mother straightened in her chair and tried to affect a disinterested mien. "I do not think you can give credit to any rumor you overhear, Alasdair. From all accounts, she has been living at Hadley House for the past six years and has not sojourned to London. No doubt any gossip would be from the jealous harpies who saw the marked attention you showed her."

Six years, was that how long she had been without sight? The weak feeling which travelled through him was abhorrent. He affected a casual smile for the benefit of his mother. "I spoke with Lord Bancroft last night. As you know, he is a close acquaintance of the family. Our conversation invariably turned to the beautiful Lady Willow."

Alasdair watched the wheels turning in his mother's head, and he swallowed the chuckle as a flush rose in her cheeks.

"Salacious gossip?" she queried, pouring herself a cup of tea from the trolley.

Salacious? He strolled over to sit beside her on the chaise lounge.

"No. Bancroft referred to the fact Lady Willow is without a dowry, and all of London is aware of it."

Her face whitened. "What utter balderdash! The Duke of Milton is wealthy and certainly not hard up for money. I would have heard of this."

She searched his expression frantically before closing her eyes. It took a few moments before she composed herself, then she opened her lids. "I can see from your face the rumors are true. If she is really dowerless, Alasdair, please strike a connection with her from your thoughts."

How easy the tides were turned.

"I never indicated such a desire on my part." Though now he was undoubtedly interested. But not to marry Willow or even to take the pleasures he had desperately wanted to pursue last night. He had a burning desire to understand the flash of pain that had clouded her gaze, to know how she had been hurt and why. While he would never marry her, they could possibly become friends.

"You could have been forced to marry her if it had been thought you compromised her!" his mother said in a strangled voice. "Why did you take a turn with Lady Willow in the gardens?"

"I do not believe I have to explain myself to you, madam."

His mother flushed, then narrowed her eyes at him. "You were always the difficult one, and I can see you are shaping up to be so now."

"Ah…Is it now the time to remind me what a disappointment I am to you and the family?"

She blanched. "Don't you ever utter such nonsense, Alasdair. You were always different from your brothers. You did not cling to me as they did, but never have I ever regretted you. Never. You are an honorable man, and I am proud you are my son."

Her voice rang with sincerity, and the feelings of warmth pouring through his chest surprised him.

"I know you felt some regard for her once, but do not pursue a woman who cannot help this family," his mother urged. "Her lack of sight is bad enough, but to be without a dowry cannot be overlooked."

A few years ago, Lady Willow was to marry the Duke of Salop. She herself had said as much. Nothing about her had changed except her sight and possibly fortune, yet as a duke's daughter, she was no longer good enough for him, in his mother's eyes, and if he was not mistaken, in Society's eyes. Alasdair waited for satisfaction to fill him. Yet he did not feel such emotions. Instead, he felt disgusted at their shallowness. A woman was so much more than her money. He hoped his sisters would find men who would cherish them, whether he was able to provide them with dowries or not.

"Alasdair," his mother said sharply at his silence. "Surely you remember your past with Lady Willow."

How could he forget?

He had wanted her from the moment he had laid eyes on her seven years ago. Though Westerham Park bordered Hadley House, Lady Willow had spent most of her time at her father's seat in Hertfordshire. It had only been as her family prepared her for the season, the Miltons had moved closer to London. Though Quinton had spent years regaling Alasdair of Willow's exploits, he had never met her until she had snuck away from her lessons to spy on her brothers at the lake and had slipped down the loose embankment from her hiding place to fall into the water.

Alasdair had dragged her out, to her utter mortification. He had forgotten how to breathe, how to blink or move when she had emerged from the water sputtering. She had been sixteen at the time, young and lovely, a spitfire, especially when she tilted her head and jutted her chin in that stubborn way of hers. Willow had been the loveliest of girls, warm, kind, high spirited, and so genuinely caring, it had not taken him long to fall in love with her.

Several days he had ridden away from Westerham Park to meet her by the lake. Simply basking in the knowledge of something sweet building between them. They had skipped stones across the lake and regaled each other with childhood anecdotes. He had taught her how to swim, against Quinton's wishes, how to ride without a mounting block and side saddle, and she had taught him how to play chess, how to appreciate the poets, how to use his fingers to trill as the nightingales do.

After spending months with her, breathing in

her laughter and love for life, she had taught him love. Then heartbreak and pain. Yet it had been memories of her which had kept him sane during the horrors of war and made him fight hard to be able to return.

And he now knew, he would not be able to stay away from her. Once again, he was a damn fool, but for some reason, he was more than happy with being a fool today.

CHAPTER 4

"The rumors say the Marquess of Westcliffe is seeking a wife," the Dowager Countess, Willow's grandmother, said from her position on the chaise. After their brief morning walk in the garden and the estate grounds, a light spatter of rain had forced them to the drawing room where they continued their conversation. To Willow's chagrin, her grandmother had mentioned her mishap the night before with amusement.

"What do you think of him, child?"

She grimaced. Had her grandmother forgotten Willow knew him? That everything she now suffered was because of the love she held for Alasdair? A rush of anger burned through her, and she fought to suppress it. No, her grandmother remembered. Alasdair was no longer a mere third son, and she would have noted his attentions last night. As far as her family was concerned, he was now suitable.

The softest of sighs escaped Willow's lips. Since their encounter, all she could think about was him, and the promise he had made in anger. Being intimate with someone was not something she had thought remotely possible, and for it to be Alasdair was more incredible than the thought of a dancing elephant. When he had taken control of her impetuous kiss, her heart had stopped, her world had narrowed, and the sweetest feeling of delight had uncurled inside of her.

With all the love she had felt for Alasdair, he had only ever kissed her once. It had been the eve of her seventeenth birthday celebration, and she had been about to leave for London for the season with her mother and aunt. When he'd heard, he had taken her to walk by the lake where they'd spent the day, huddled in the cold, talking of impossible dreams.

You make me happy, Willow. I make you happy. Do not leave. Marry me.

His words had been simple, without artful flattery and phrases, but a knowing had shifted inside of her, a kindred feeling, and a surge of love so intense fear had shaken her. Since their meeting the summer before, every moment with him had been blissful, and she had bitterly regretted the need to part from him, to plunge into the marriage mart. He was the one she had desired, but she had known her father would never accept his offer.

THEN NOT EVEN A WEEK LATER, her father informed her he accepted the Duke of Salop's offer for her hand in marriage. She still remembered the rage on her father's face when she had threatened to run away with Alasdair. Her father had slapped her, and the cold violence and rage behind his actions had petrified Willow. He had apologized immediately and enfolded her in a hug, then had made the chilling promise that Alasdair would regret loving her, for her father would ruin him if she ran away and married beneath her station. She had believed her father. Nothing of the rage he had shown before had been present, only an icy purpose.

It was her mother who had fully persuaded Willow a third son would not be able to offer her the comforts of life that she had been privileged to experience, and if she continued to be adamant in wanting to marry Alasdair, her father would ruin him. Alasdair's family had already been on the brink of financial disaster with his father's gambling, and her mother had pointed out it would not take much for her father, a powerful and respected duke to drive the final nail in the coffin of the Westcliffe family. The loss of comfort her mother had spoken of, the loss of jewelries, clothes, and the best carriages had not affected Willow much. But the fear her father would crush every ambition of Alasdair's had been daunting. The maelstrom of emotions the memory evoked rattled her, and she pushed the past from her mind.

"Would you agree, child, that the Marquess of Westcliffe is a suitable match?"

Willow wanted to scream. Why was her grandmother asking her this? Of course, he would be more than suitable, but what would that be to her? She now had the inferior circumstances. She was flawed. She was dowerless. And from all he had said the night before, he only wanted to bury his cock in her, to exorcise her from his dreams. Heat climbed her cheeks.

At the tender age of fifteen, she had caught her brother Quinton naked with his limbs entwined with her governess. They had undulated together in the most sensual of rhythms. The shock of it had stayed with Willow for years, but she had a good idea of what Alasdair referred to when he said he wanted to be buried in her. The curl of heat that surged through her at the thought of them naked, sweating together, her begging and clawing his back as he promised had her mouth drying.

"Willow?"

The pique in her grandmother's tone was evident. With a sigh Willow directed her thoughts to their conversation. "I am without dowry... without sight, and I rejected him years ago when I had all of this, Grandmother. He will not be persuaded now to accept me."

Her parents believed they were protecting her by rendering her penniless, but they placed her in the untenable situation of being unsuitable for any gentleman. She was already an encumbrance without her sight, but to have no money? To come to any marriage only as a burden?

She had argued with her father. Her brothers had pleaded with him to reconsider, but the duke had been firm. She would remain without a dowry. Of course, all of this occurred because of that blasted poppycock James Bailey, the Earl of

Trenton. He had pursued her so ardently, despite her blindness, and she had felt some hope that a gentleman would see her as more than an unwanted wife. But it had all been about her wealth. Lord Trenton had easily departed after her father explained he would only provide a thousand pound for her dowry. Trenton had failed her father's test, and Willow had been shattered. She had liked and respected Lord Trenton and believed she could have been comfortably situated. But the fearful reality she had been hiding from, had crashed into her with brutal precision.

"You do not give much credit to your beauty, my dear. I observed when Lord Westcliffe came to your rescue last night. I made the decision not to intervene from the way he looked at you," her grandmother said at Willow's silence.

Her throat felt tight and aching, but she pushed the words passed her lips. "I think it convenient for you to pretend, Grandmother, that I had not rejected him and hurt him abominably. Why should he now be amenable toward me, because I now recognize he has a title? Either way, I am no longer interested in the institution of marriage."

Never would she be a burden to a man who

would certainly grow to resent her, even if her dowry had been considerable.

"You are foolish, my dear. You need your own family. You cannot spend the rest of your life secreted at Hadley House. While my daughter expects to smother and hover over you for the remainder of her life, I expect you to live, to remain stalwart in the strength you have displayed since you were a babe. Do you not desire more?"

Yes, she wanted pleasure, passion. To feel Alasdair on top of her, inside her, kissing her, and drowning her with sensation she was sure to never feel again even if she married elsewhere. Her heart clamored when she admitted her scandalous thoughts to herself. She had tasted such delights at last night's ball, and she wanted more.

She raised her fingers to her lips. The flavor of him still lingered. A wistful sigh escaped her lips. She desired to feel that slow slide into bliss again, to feel the rise of passion as it consumed her. And she wanted to experience it with Alasdair. But even if some miracle were to occur where he would indeed desire her to be his wife, she would never saddle him with a blind marchioness. "Grandmother…"

"Yes?"

She hesitated, fighting the blush.

"What is it, Willow?" Gentle understanding was rife in her tone.

"What does he look like?"

There was a pulse of painful silence before the dowager countess spoke, "Lord Westcliffe?"

She cleared her throat. "Yes."

"He is still very handsome. He appears a bit different from what you would remember. The flush of youth is gone, and he looks harder…a bit colder. I think the effects of the war. His efforts have been much lauded, and many nights that is all your father and Quinton discuss."

Pride curled through Willow. "Thank you. Do you know what happened to his brothers?"

"Do you not think that is a question for the marquess? It would give you something to converse about."

"Grandmother, please." Willow did not hide the exasperation in her tone.

There was a knock on the door, and her grandmother's impervious voice bid entrance.

Dawson, their butler came in. "There is a caller for Lady Willow," he murmured.

Her heart leaped. Without Dawson saying it, she knew it was Alasdair.

"Lord Westcliffe, my lady."

"Indeed?" her grandmother said archly, but Willow could hear the deep satisfaction in her voice. "Please show him into the drawing room and order refreshments."

Willow turned from the open windows, walking ten paces toward the chaise in the left corner. She sat questions bubbling inside, waiting for Alasdair to enter. Was he interested in courting her? After the way she had treated him? He had no idea of the foolish and devastating lengths she had endured to reach him, to recant her words and profess her adoration for him. So why would he be showing her any attention now?

Repayment.

The thought had her breath halting. What if he wanted atonement for the way she had dismissed his love? She would never forget the flash of agony on his face when she had told him, she was to marry another, and he should forget her. His expression had reflected all the hopeless torment she had felt inside, from bowing to her family's persuasion. It mattered not to her that in her reckless bid to make amends, she had been hurt on such a debilitating level. He did not know of her efforts, and she would never tell him.

Last night proved she had enjoyed his lust, his

passion, and while she might even suffer his anger…she did not want his pity. And what she would admit was that she needed his desire. Needed to feel alive after the years of unending loneliness. And while she would never consent to be anyone's wife…she would take a leap, for a taste of desire.

CHAPTER 5

Alasdair invited her to picnic by the lake and then to swim.

Something so ordinary should never have caused the panic that had bled from her mother's voice when Willow informed her of his request, and Willow had not even told her of the swimming part. He had said it teasingly, with a sensual promise of more in his tone.

That more had intrigued her, and she wanted to be alone with him for the day.

The duchess had been deaf to Willow's firm stance that she was three and twenty and it was perfectly safe to picnic with a childhood friend. Her mother had spluttered at the impropriety of walking with Alasdair without a chaperone. Willow was grateful her father and brothers were in London, for she would not have been able to defeat their strong objections, to being with him by herself. She was no longer the girl of sixteen who had been allowed too much freedom with Alasdair.

It was Grandmother who had gently encouraged Willow's mother to let her be. But her mother had only relented after Willow agreed to take Olivia as a chaperone. And yet her mother was still not satisfied.

Willow loved her mother, but her overprotectiveness was tiring.

"Willow—"

"Please, Mother." She smiled to remove the sting of her words. "Allow me this without an argument. The weather is perfect, and I have not been to the lake for almost a year. Father stifles me, and though Quinton and Grayson try to be different, they are rather much the same."

"You will ensure Oliva is with you at all times," her mother said.

Willow smiled noncommittally. She had no intention of taking Olivia with her, not when the promise of passion had been so evident in Alasdair's tone. Willow would allow ample opportunities for him to steal a kiss again if he so desired.

A heavy sigh slipped from her mother, then there was a rustle of sound, and the smell of peaches and lemons wafted closer. Her mother's fragrance had always been comforting, unique. Willow turned toward her mother, reaching out her hands.

The lightest of kisses brushed her cheek, and she could smell the faint tang of sherry on her mother's breath. "You have been drinking."

"Do not concern yourself, it was only one glass. Go and have a pleasant time. Though I may need another glass to fortify my nerves when your father discovers I allowed this. I am sure he would have wanted to speak with Lord Westcliffe before he allowed any courtship."

Willow did not point out it was barely noon, much too early for her mother to be imbibing, and she certainty did not mention this was not a courtship. "Thank you, Mother." She returned her mother's embrace.

Willow walked from the drawing room without assistance to her chambers up the winding stairs. With the aid of her lady's maid, Anne, Willow dressed in a simple walking gown. It had not taken much to convince Olivia to grant Willow privacy with the marquess. Her friend and companion understood the raging need she possessed to be unchained from her mother's stifling overprotectiveness and fear. Though Olivia had asked her to be careful, for her companion was fully aware of Willow's history with Alasdair.

"I am leaving my hair down in a plait."

"Yes, my lady," Anne murmured.

A few minutes later Willow descended the stairs fully composed, hoping none of the tearing emotions she'd felt were evident. She ran her hand along the railing, counting her steps. Halfway down, she paused. Alasdair was near. The scent of him flooded her senses. "Have you come to escort me down the stairs?"

"Impressive indeed," he said, and then a breath later he was beside her.

"Mayhap not as impressive as your scent is distinct, my lord. I will admit you move with the grace of a predator. I did not feel you come closer."

There was a subtle intake of breath. "Shall we?" he asked.

She reached out, and he guided her hand to his arm.

"We shall," she said with a light laugh. "I urge

our departure before Mother comes to her senses and makes a ruckus of me leaving with you."

"Your curricle awaits, my lady."

It seemed as if he dipped his head closer because warmth coasted near her cheeks. Scotch, chocolate, and if she was not mistaken, bilberries, an interesting combination. A slow ache curled through her. If she did not guard her emotions, she might once again receive a cruel blow from the fickle hands of fate.

Thirty minutes later, Willow listened to the lapping of the lake, the smooth rush of the water, and leaned forward from where she sat on the grass, gliding her fingertips over the lake's surface. It felt divine. They had been at the lake for almost ten minutes, and she had yet to submerge herself fully into the water. She missed swimming, she missed so many things. It would indeed be glorious to feel the water caressing her skin again, if only she were brave enough to ask Alasdair for assistance.

The smell of rain and something all too elusive wrapped itself around her. Her skin tingled with awareness, and her body came alive at Alasdair's nearness.

"How may I aid in your enjoyment of the day?" he asked softly.

She stiffened. From the ripples in the water, the soft splash, she could feel him wading closer.

"I am content to sit here and soak my feet."

She fancied she felt his puzzlement, but how could she explain she did not want to be burdensome?

"Are you? You were a quick study when I taught you to swim. I remember us meeting here almost every day for weeks. I cannot credit you would not wish to take advantage of the marvelous weather. Is it that you have been to the lake so often?"

The sun was bright, and even in her realm of almost darkness, she could see the splice of light edging the void. She berated herself for her hesitancy. "No, I walked by a few times with Quinton, but I have not swum since my accident."

"Then why will you not accept my aid?"

"Why are we here?" she asked instead of answering him.

It was a difficult thing to force their outing into perspective. She had missed him so. But she could not allow herself to believe it meant anything of substance, despite their kiss, despite her wanting him. She couldn't afford to expose herself to such hurt again. Lord Trenton, the toad, had started out admiring her, courting her before he had offered for her hand.

I am mightily exhausted of always needing to be here for you. It wears on a man, Willow.

When he had snapped those words with evident frustration, she had been shattered, believing she had been doing so well at self-sufficiency. Then she'd realized she was only self-sufficient at Hadley House. There she knew every nook and cranny, every gravel path and garden, and the length and depth of the lake. She had sprained an ankle and had received several bruises in her determination to learn the property.

Hadley House was her prison…and also her freedom.

She'd recollected how much he had to assist her once they were away from Hadley House. First, he had been caring. Solicitous, gentle even, then it had slowly turned to brusqueness and anger. Lord Trenton had convinced himself to continue because he needed her money.

She must never read anything into Alasdair inviting her out. They had been friends, and she must be careful to not love him so desperately again. She would not be able to bear his distaste, which was an eventuality. *Do not forget he left…and never once looked back.* The dark part of her she had struggled to defeat reared its head. She swallowed the bitterness and dwelt in the moment itself. She had rejected him. It mattered not that she regretted that decision. He was not to blame for anything she suffered.

Willow closed her eyes against the painful memories. "Will you not answer my question? Why did you call on me today?"

"I am here because I desire to reacquaint myself with you. I have no nefarious reasons."

So he had abandoned his plans of seduction? Disappointment stabbed through her. "I see," she said quietly.

"Do you think I would hurt you?"

She frowned at his unexpected question. "I—"

He chuckled. "You are very transparent with your emotions. I can see your wariness. But I promise you, I will not hurt you." Sincerity rang in his voice.

"And your vow to exorcise me from your dreams?"

She heard him drifting closer.

"I assure you that is not my intention today. The shock of seeing you for the first time in years last night prompted my unchivalrous actions. You are safe with me, I promise, Willow."

"How disappointing," she said softy. She had hoped to indulge in passion again today.

"You are disappointed I am not ravishing you?" His voice was carefully neutral.

She shrugged indelicately. "I will confess I have been thinking about you as a lover."

A soft curse slipped from him, and a blush heated her cheeks. But she would not retract the words. Life was too fleeting for her to hesitate with her desires. She wanted more, and he was the man she had craved for years. Who better to experience passion with?

"I do not think your future husband would appreciate your sentiments."

"Since I have no intention of ever marrying, I think your point is irrelevant. I am interested in a discreet affair...with you, Alasdair."

His stare was so intense it was a heated caress against her skin.

"I can feel you staring," she said huskily.

"Join me in the water," he invited, and it was the deep undertone of need in his voice that lured her.

Willow stood, and without hesitation slipped out

of the simple day dress, standing in her chemisette. He swore softly, and her pulse quickened. She lowered herself onto the banking, and slowly eased into the lake.

The gasp was trapped in her throat as firm hands gripped her hips and gently lifted her, sinking her to the waist in the water. Cool water rushed over her soaking her chemisette. She wrapped one of her arms around his neck and placed the other on his shoulder. The sensation of the water was glorious, but not as much as the feel of his strength and the muscles in his shoulders. Her hand coasted over his naked flesh almost reverently. She had not thought he would have stripped to the waist.

"I think you were placed on earth to tempt my sanity," he murmured. Amusement laced his tone. "I vowed not to take you, yet all I can think since you professed of wanting me as a lover is to spread you wide, feast on your sweetness, then ride you until we are both boneless with pleasure."

She gasped at the raw desire his words elicited. Her body felt suffused with heat, and she was embarrassed to acknowledge she was at a loss for words. "Then take me," she pushed the words past her lips.

His silence unnerved her. What was he thinking? "What are—?"

"Why are you not married to Salop?"

She stiffened, then forced her limbs to relax. "Our agreement was cancelled by my father after my accident. Salop did not object."

The muscles in his shoulders twisted as he waded further out into the lake with her. "I see. Did you love him?"

"Why are you asking me this?"

"Did you love him, Willow?" he demanded softly.

She shook her head. "I have only ever felt such depth of affections for you," she admitted without any reservation. She had never been ashamed of how she felt about Alasdair.

A soft kiss brushed against her lips, then he spoke, "Trust me for today. Relax with me. Let me be your guide in the water. Let us converse and relearn each other."

She nodded, absurdly pleased with the idea of learning everything about him. "You should know I am not interested in marriage."

Tension shifted through his frame, and the fingers still holding her hips tightened on her flesh perceptibly.

"I do not believe I mentioned marriage."

Curiosity filled her. "You are comfortable with us having an affair?"

"Though I think of nothing but you, your smiles, and your lushly curved body, I will not take you. You deserve better than a quick romp, or to be a mistress."

Amusement curled though her. "I cannot remember offering to be your mistress."

His arms came around her, and he spun them, taking her deeper until the water rose to her chest. "You tempt me so damn much," he said roughly. "Wrap your legs around my waist."

She complied and encountered a rigid hardness that caused the sweetest throb in her center. She moaned deep in her throat as he pulled her closer, rubbing against a spot that caused her to almost jackknife away from him so intense was the pleasure. His hands slid up her side to gently cup the underside of her breasts.

Palpable sensual tension arced between them. "Kiss me, Alasdair."

"No."

She wriggled, he hissed and pulled her even firmer against the hard ridge of his arousal. The valley between her thighs throbbed with startling intensity. Impatience bit at her and Willow released his shoulders and slid her hands through his damp hair. She grabbed a fistful and tugged lower.

He laughed, and she leaned forward and bit his chin.

"Bold, aren't you?"

She licked the spot she bit, and he went still. She then placed a soft kiss on the corner of his mouth and trailed kisses to his ear, so there could be no doubt of her words. "I desire you to touch me, to kiss me, because I crave something more in my life. I want this ache between my legs to be filled." She snaked one of her hands between them, shifted a bit to create space, and cupped his hardness.

He groaned, and she smiled.

"This is what I want to fill me. Not because of the past and pain that still lies between us, and not because I feel fear. But because I feel something more than fear and doubt for the first time in years, and I only feel that with you." She paused and squeezed his thick length harder.

"I am not seeking a quick romp, or to be your mistress. I am seeking pleasures with a man I trust to be gentle and kind. If you'll eventually desire marriage for besmirching my honor, walk away, for

I will not consent to anything greater than this burning passion."

Silence. God awful silence at her declaration and Willow desperately wished she could see his features. A lump grew in her throat.

Then he leaned close, so close their lips brushed, and whispered, "Take a deep breath."

CHAPTER 6

E very emotion Willow felt was reflected in her eyes. He had seen her doubts at his silence, her passion when experiencing his touch, and her slow outrage at his whispered 'Take a deep breath.' But Alasdair did not hesitate. He lifted and dumped her deeper into the water. Though she spoke with such certainty of her desire, artlessness glowed around her, and her air of innocence was wonderfully alluring.

She rose sputtering, her cheeks darkening, eyes narrowed. Water dripped from her hair, and some of the tendrils snaked from her plait. She looked too damn appealing. Submerging himself fully into the water did nothing to curb the ardor she roused in him.

"You cretin."

Her feminine outrage growled at him, only inflamed him further. He dived deep, swimming toward her, and pulled her legs from underneath her. She moved like a dream under the water as she twisted, sliding against him to rise to the surface. Her eyes widened, and then a shout of laughter slipped from her. Her laughter was charming, impossible to resist, and he found himself responding. It was also the most enjoyable sound he had heard in a long time. But he had accomplished something. The doubt that had lingered in her eyes, even when she spoke so boldly of taking him, had melted away.

"I am to your left."

She swam toward him before he finished speaking. Her sense of hearing and perception amazed him.

"I can see from your playfulness you have no intention of indulging in pleasures today."

He grunted, and she grinned.

"You love the water, being outdoors. Why did you stop swimming?"

She went silent, gazing at him in that piercing way as if she could see him. Her shoulders relaxed, and she swam lazily to him. "I did not stop. My parents stopped me. I think it was from fear of losing me."

He met her halfway and drew her to his side, drifting with her along the currents. An ache filled his chest as she complied, seamlessly gliding through the water beside him. It meant she trusted him.

A rueful smile curved her lips. "Pray do not believe I did not wallow in self-pity for years. I did. For two years, I hardly left my room, closing myself off from everyone. The horror of what I had lost drowned me for a long time."

"Then what happened?" he asked quietly, imagining the pain and isolation she must have endured.

She flipped on her back and started to float. "I got irritated with myself. I was a bear to everyone. In the first few months, I yelled, and I threw tantrums. I refused to eat, bathe, everything was a battle to those people who only wanted me to be happy, as happy as I could be given my circumstances. I emerged from my self-imposed prison, and then I realized how much my wings had been clipped. While I had the freedom to roam the house, which I did so many times that I can walk now unassisted, the fear my mother felt at me moving beyond the garden has grounded me to the estate, away from our lake," she ended wistfully.

He glanced at her as she lazed on the surface of the water, the sun glistening off her skin. A deep need to please her scythed through his heart, and he pushed away the desire. If he allowed himself to care for her, it would be a disaster. Though he enjoyed himself more than he could recall in his life, he never forgot that he must wed an heiress. His mother had presented him with several candidates before he left Westerham Park.

His intentions today were simply about being in Willow's presence. He was startled to realize most of his anger had faded away. Knowing how she suffered, made Alasdair felt tormented. He cared. He had only to look at her and his pulse raced. He liked it. He felt something other than loneliness, a fatal sense of duty, and obligation. "Will you tell me how you lost your sight?" he invited, desperately wanting to know.

She was silent for the longest time. "I fell from a horse. The blow to my head detached my retinas. The doctors said nothing can be done."

Fell from a horse? She was an expert horsewoman. He had even taught her to ride without a side saddle. "How did—"

"No. I told you how. No more."

She twisted, sliding against him before he could say more, and found his lips with unerring accuracy. It was a fleeting kiss, one filled with more teasing than real passion. She trailed her lips to his jawline.

Her womanly fragrance overwhelmed him, intoxicating his senses. She turned her face into his neck, inhaled his scent, and then pressed a lingering kiss there. He swore. Need rocketed through him from that simple caress.

What in damnation was he doing? She was wholly unsuitable to be his bride, yet he was taking liberties. It hardly mattered she was the one doing the touching. He would never really make love to her and then abandon her. It certainly made no sense to linger on the memory of her taste or the lushness of her lips. If only he could burn from his mind what her face looked like suffused with pleasure.

She deserved more. She spoke of only wanting passion, but he instinctively realized it was fear that pushed her to such thoughts. In the past, laughing and frolicking with each other by this very lake, she had confessed to wanting a large family.

"How did your accident happen?"

She stiffened and moved with graceful strokes

away from him. He did not allow her to retreat but sliced through the water, deliberately crowding her space, guiding her to lean against a rock near the embankment.

"Willow?" he prompted at her continued silence.

"I was acting foolishly and pushed my horse too fast."

Her face was a cool mask, but he detected something painful in her tone.

"I am deeply regretful you felt such pain."

She nodded and offered him a wobbly smile.

"When was this?"

"A long time ago."

He arched a brow and examined her closely, doing his best to keep his gaze above her neck. Her chemisette was pasted to the ripe curves of her body, and since they'd been swimming, he had even resorted to reciting Latin to keep his mind from the gutter. "Whatever happened must have been in the year you and I parted. What happened, Willow?"

She huffed an impatient breath. "This line of questioning is over. There is only one thing left for us to discuss today, my lord."

For some reason, he was no longer turned off from hearing the reminder of his title on her lips.

"And that is?" Though he knew from the sensuality suffusing her face.

Her touch, so delicate, uncertain even, yet so seductive, drifted over his chest. "I would like to appease my curiosity."

"A curiosity, am I?"

There was a pulse of silence that seethed with more than lust.

"You would also be a memory, one I can recall when all else is dark, and loneliness eats at my soul," she admitted with a frankness that startled him.

From the flush that climbed her cheeks, he deduced she had not meant to be so forthcoming either. And at that moment, he knew he would grant her what she wished for, and indulge in what he had hungered for, for so many years.

❧❧❧

THE HARD CHEST beneath her hands rippled with power. Alasdair had always been graceful, athletic. He was muscled with broad, defined shoulders. She glided the tip of her finger over the sharp sensual angles of his jaw, up to his hair. The strands of his hair were soft and curled around her fingertips. Images of his gray eyes floated in her mind, and she prayed she would never forget the heat that used to dwell within whenever his gaze had turned to hers.

Warm hands cupped her cheeks, and she shifted her neck slightly and placed a kiss toward his palm. It landed on his knuckles. His fractured breathing rippled through her, pushing away the uncertainty. "I cannot resist you, Willow. Years later and I still cannot resist you."

Her breath hitched at the raw need in his voice. She also heard the bleakness underneath the layer of desire. "I do not want you to resist. In the past six years, a night has not gone by that I did not think of you," she breathed huskily, sliding her hand down his chest to his stomach. She was pleased to feel the muscular wall of his abdomen contracting at her caress. The slightly rougher texture of his flesh had her pausing. "What is this?"

"A scar, from the war."

She traced the puckered flesh with the tip of her finger. "I am sorry you were hurt. Will you tell me about it?"

"Yes." He inhaled sharply when she dipped her hand lower to tease along his waistline.

Alasdair gripped her hand to keep her from exploring further, drew her roughly against his body and claimed her lips.

Sweet glorious heaven.

There was nothing teasing or gentle about his claiming. Everything faded. The birds trilling in the distance, the soft sound of the water as it lapped at their heated bodies. He kissed her until she was weak and shivering in his arms until she was intoxicated by the pleasure of his taste. He traced the contours of her back, down to her buttocks, and drew her closer to his hardness.

"Yes," she gasped, never wanting the chaotic sensations engulfing her body to stop.

Alasdair's fingers glided over her knees up to her thighs to find the source of her heat with aching precision. He stroked across her knot of pleasure, streaking agonizing need through her body. She shifted, clamping her thighs tighter around his hips.

With a groan against her lips, he slipped his fingers down and glided one deep inside her. She sobbed into his mouth, shaking at the fire pulsing between her thighs. Every touch of his hand and every movement of his body against her took her deeper and deeper in want...into desire.

"Please," she whispered, her voice broken. "I crave something more." What, she didn't know, but she needed. "Make me burn, Alasdair."

She felt his loss of control as he roughly

widened his stance, opening her more to his intimate touch. She bit his lip as he pressed deeper, his thumb circling her knot of pleasure in time to the two fingers now plunging into her core. *Oh God.* He kissed her harder his tongue moving in symphony to the sensual thrusts between her legs.

The sweetest of pain and pleasure combined into burning ecstasy and a wave of heat rolled over her. She moaned, tearing her mouth from his, burying her face in his neck as sheer bliss consumed her, leaving her shaking and clasping his shoulders.

Alasdair waded with her to the shallow end, unwrapping her legs from his waist to place her on the grassy knoll, blanketing her body with his. He was larger than she remembered. A frisson of awareness and lust pierced her. She should have felt vulnerable at his obvious strength, instead exhilaration shot through her. He caressed her shoulders, down to her side with untamed hunger. He pressed a gentle kiss to her lips, while one of his hands pushed her chemisette to her waist.

He cupped her core, pressing his palm with gentle force against her nub.

Sweet Lord.

A delicious wave of needed roiled through her body. "You promised to make me ache relentlessly.

What are you waiting for?" she demanded nipping his bottom lips softly.

A groan pulsed from him, and a smile of satisfaction creased her lips. She loved that she affected him as much.

"No," she gasped as he withdrew from her, pulling her chemisette down. "Why did you stop?"

"With you, I have no control. I will not make love with you for the first time here. I will have you in my bed where I can worship your body as you deserve," he said, almost reverently.

A sensual smile curved her lips, and she lifted her face to his. "Kiss me," she invited.

"What the blasted hell is going on?"

The snarl of rage had her freezing in shock. Alasdair rolled from her in one smooth motion.

Willow trembled. *Who was it?*

"Easy," Alasdair murmured when she scrambled to her feet. "He saw nothing."

"Unhand my sister, Westcliffe." The voice was stiff with anger.

She felt Alasdair's heat retreating.

It was Quinton. Why was he here? He should be in London with Grayson and her father. Her knees wobbled. She was compromised. She would not wed Alasdair under these circumstances, under any circumstance. How could she have been so reckless? While she knew the lake was exposed, no one visited at this time of the day.

The cool breeze that wafted over her skin had a shiver skating over her body.

A scent of tobacco and oak moss drifted close, and then rough hands started to dry her hair.

"Do not make the error of bruising her skin because you are angry," Alasdair warned. The cold rebuke in his voice was startling. The command in it had her brother stiffening, but he halted his rough actions.

"Thank you," she said softly.

She had always been closer to Quinton than Grayson, and she could only imagine the anger Quinton must be feeling at the thought she had been taken advantage of. He had been the one to punch Lord Trenton for his behavior. He had been the one to encourage her the most to be brave and fight to be independent of their family's overprotectiveness.

"He did not take advantage of me, Quinton. It was I who was bold and inappropriate."

"Be quiet Willow, I will speak with Quinton."

She ignored Alasdair's command. "I will not have my brothers and father force you to do what they believe is honorable. If he had remained in London, there would be no ruckus."

"Devil take it, Willow, this is serious business," Quinton snapped.

A blanket was draped over her, and she clutched it close.

"It is only dire if you make it out to be. I ask you to keep our confidence, Quinton. I would not want father to know what you witnessed."

Virulent curses slipped from his lips. "I will take you home."

"Quinton—" Alasdair began.

"No, Westcliffe, I know your position, and I am aware of what you are seeking. She is my goddamn sister, and you knew you were not up to scratch."

She stiffened. The rage in her brother's tone had apprehension skittering up her spine. What did he know about Alasdair?

"Do you believe you could ride on my horse?" Quinton asked her.

Her head swam. "No," she managed to push the words past her lips. He knew she had never been able to seat herself on a horse since her accident. "Take the curricle," Alasdair offered quietly. "I will walk back."

She felt the tension that snapped between the

men and regretted it. They had been the closest of friends as long as she could remember. She would need to speak with Quinton, so he understood this was her decision, and she had not been coerced. For a sense of doom had been twisting inside of her since his appearance. He would try to force her to do the right thing, the honorable thing. But he and her family would never understand that is exactly what she would be doing when she rejected the offer of marriage that was sure to come.

CHAPTER 7

"What the hell were you thinking?" Quinton snarled hours later as he strode into Alasdair's library.

He had known what was coming and had been deep in thoughts. The emotions Willow roused in him were similar to those he had formerly felt, except now he saw her through the viewpoint of a man. There was a time Alasdair had been convinced, once he experienced pleasure in Willow's arms, the desperate hunger he had felt for her over the years would ease. He grimaced. It had increased tenfold. She haunted his most wicked and sensual dreams. He wanted her. And not only for pleasure. He wanted her as his marchioness.

He had swiftly composed letters to his solicitor,

his barrister, his investment partners, and the stewards of his estates. He wanted to understand his financial standing and how long he would remain solvent if he married her.

The doubts crowded his mind. Could he still pursue Willow and achieve happiness for his sisters? They needed him, and their disappointment he would not bear. He wanted to smash the glass of brandy into the wall above the fireplace.

"Well?" his friend demanded.

Alasdair asked, "Is Willow well?"

Quinton sighed. "As well as can be. Our grandmother realized something was amiss, and I stupidly confided in her. The alacrity in which she told our father you had compromised Willow startled me."

Alasdair braced himself. "How did Willow react to that?"

Quinton came to stand beside him, still stiff with anger. "She has told our father she will not be forced into misery."

Alasdair jerked, and from the sharp glance of his friend, he surmised he had not masked his reaction. The pain of her words sliced deep. But what had he expected? She had been right when she accused him of leaving and not looking back.

Though it had not been intentional. His father's death, his mother's grief, and Marcus's illness had all happened within months of each other. It had been a lot to deal with. The despair of those times still had the power to affect Alasdair even after all these years. But when he finally emerged from the shadow of it all, he had not looked behind him, assuming that she had married her duke.

What a damn fool he had been.

"It is not you Willow objects to my friend," Quinton admitted. "It is the situation. She fears to be a burden. Though it is embarrassing to admit, I saw her face as she smiled at you. I realize nothing has changed for her, even after six years. She holds the same regard for you, and it is that regard that will make her deny you. Even as father roared, she only sought to protect you from his anger."

"I can manage the duke's wrath."

Quinton sighed. "I told her as much. Why would you place yourself in such a situation?"

Alasdair ignored the question. "She told me she fell from her horse."

His friend was silent for the longest time.

"What happened, Quinton? Please tell me."

"She rode after you."

Alasdair stiffened, a deep sense of foreboding filling his chest. "What do you mean?"

"I overheard her rejection of your offer."

My father has forbidden our union. You are only a third son, and he believes I deserve more. You say you are leaving for Europe. Go. I won't change my opinion.

While the memory still stung, the words no longer choked him with loss as they once did.

"She cried for days in her room after you left. Our parents were proud of her. Hell, everyone thought she was being sensible, but she was miserable. I visited her and asked her if she loved you. I regret to this day I interfered. For when she said yes, I told her the truth, that in a few hours, you would leave London and it could be years before you returned. She rushed to our father, confessed her love and expressed only wanting to be with you, and that she needed to visit you. Her request for the carriage and chaperone was denied. She went to the stables, mounted her horse and rode for Westerham Park."

"Hell!"

He glanced at Quinton and the savage fury and pain on his face told the rest of the story.

"Grayson is more tormented than I am. He has never been the same, and the wild debauchery he indulges in now is to soothe his guilt. He was the one that rode after her…to stop her. She urged her horse faster when she realized he was on her trail. She was thrown. I was following behind him, and I do not think I will ever forget his cry of fear when he realized what had happened. We raced to her side, and she was unconscious, bleeding from the head. The next two weeks were the most terrified I had ever been in my life, not even what we experienced in the war compared."

There was an empty, hollow ache in Alasdair's chest. It was his fault she was blind. The guilt crashed into him like a wave, suffocating and drowning him. All these years while he had raged at her, believing her fickle, she had raced after him and had been hurt. He logically tried to wade through the pain. It had been years ago, and to allow the grip of guilt to warp his mind now would be foolhardy. "You should have told me," he said softly.

Quinton sighed. "Maybe. But what would you have done? Run to her side and offered to be with her out of guilt?"

"No…I loved her, I wouldn't have needed chains of guilt. I would have cared for her, been there when the doubts ravaged her, and when she felt alone in her world…I would have supported her."

Quinton smiled grimly. "I think it best you were absent, the first few years were very torturing for her. It has only been these past couple years I have seen my sister gain some peace."

Alasdair probably shouldn't torment himself further, but he needed to know. "Did she call for me?"

His friend ran his fingers through the thick strands of his dark hair and grimaced. "Yes, for days."

Alasdair flinched.

"It was stories of you that kept her sane and allowed her to fight for life."

"Why did you never tell me?" he demanded hoarsely. "Why? We are friends, Quinton. You knew how I felt about Willow."

He would never have been in any doubt. Alasdair had professed years ago with a simple declaration of 'I love your sister, and I'm going to marry her. I will endeavor to provide for her so that she will never want for anything. I swear to you.'

It had been Alasdair's way of declaring his intention to the one person whose opinion truly mattered to him.

"She was blinded Al…blinded and broken."

The depth of fury that rocketed through Alasdair's heart shocked him. "This is your opinion of me? You think me so shallow I would stay away from the woman I love more than life because of blindness? That I would have stayed away because she could not see?" he snarled.

A pained look swirled in the depth of Quinton's eyes. "I realized quite late the depth of your affections. You were both so young. Willow was sixteen when you met her, and you were twenty. After her rejection, you left England for several months. I thought that meant the affections you felt for her were fleeting. It was only in the Peninsula I truly understood the love you held for her, and that you left, because you wouldn't have been able to endure seeing her in Society on another man's arm."

War. The memories crowded Alasdair's mind. The stench of blood, the feel of despair, the burn of the agonizing pain as the bullet had lodged itself in his stomach. A wound he should have died from. But Quinton had anchored him to life by simply telling him of Willow.

Hell. "And now? What is your opinion now?"

His friend sighed. "Though I know the love

between you, it is hard for me not to smash your teeth in. You were leaning over my sister."

Quinton shot him a furious glare and Alasdair was startled to feel the tip of his ears burning. His loss of control had been witnessed. Never had he intended their embrace to traverse such a path. Quinton had only seen them after Alasdair had brought her to pleasure, inhaling the sweet scent of her desire. He was damned lucky he had not followed his wild inclination to splay her legs and kiss her deeply in her most intimate spot.

He would have surely been facing her father at dawn.

"Honor demands you marry my sister," Quinton said into the quiet of the library.

Alasdair's gut clenched. "I am not sure if I should feel happiness or despair," he murmured.

His friend threw him a curious glance. "Despair?"

Then understanding dawned into his green eyes so much like Willow's. "Even buried in Suffolk you have heard the rumors? You know that Willow is dowry less?"

Alasdair nodded in confirmation.

"You need an heiress. Your estates are in debt

by thousands. The winnings you make from gambling is not enough."

Quinton walked over to the mantle and poured whisky into two glasses. "Why in God's name did you pursue my sister, if you knew she had no money upon marriage? I have spoken to father several times, and I assure you, he will not unbend on his stance."

Alasdair took a swallow of his drink, appreciating the fire that trailed down his throat. "I was not pursuing her. I merely invited her for an outing. I was desperate to fill the need in me to know how she has fared. I never intended to lose control," he said ruefully.

"Your intention was to trifle with my sister, and then marry someone else?" Quinton asked, a dangerous undercurrent in his tone.

"No...I had no intention of even touching her."

A muscle ticked along Quinton's jaw. "So what the hell happened?"

Alasdair knew he would sound like a fool, but he still admitted it. "She laughed." And the sound had sneaked into the cold dark place where he had been dwelling and thawed him.

Quinton went silent.

Alasdair figured he didn't have to say anymore.

"You love her."

He winced at the quiet assertion. Was he so transparent? "I never stopped."

Compassion radiated from Quinton's gaze. "You are in an impossible situation, my friend. To wed my sister would surely be your family's ruin. But my grandmother will not allow any other outcome. She has already convinced my father Willow is beyond compromised by your licentious behavior. And despite knowing the debt you are in, I myself desire you to do the honorable thing."

Alasdair smiled without mirth. Honor be damned. He was willing to marry Willow, and not because they had been seen in such a scandalous position. But because he had never stopped loving her. "I will not marry Willow because of honor, but because I never stopped caring for her and from her words by the lake, I can see she would willingly deny herself happiness and a family because of fear. She had always been so vibrant, so full of life. Today I only saw a shadow of her vibrancy. It guts me to think of her alone for the rest of her life when she is loved. For years, I promised myself to never love another. And that was because Willow never left me, Quinton. I would be a fool if I gave her up a second time."

And what of your family? Your sisters who are relying on you to wed an heiress? His conscience taunted.

"And what of the money your estates need?"

Alasdair thrust his hands into his pockets and turned from the windows. "I will find a way out of my financial mess."

Or relinquish Willow.

A thing he could not bear to contemplate.

What a damn quandary. But he would do all in his power to make all the women in his life happy. He would wed Willow, convince her of his love and rid her eyes of their lingering sadness. He would also take the position with the Foreign Office, invest in lands and spices, and do his best to ensure his sisters, his mother, and estates were more than adequately cared for.

No other outcome was even possible for him to contemplate. For he would not turn his back on Willow again.

৩ঌৎৡ

STUART ARLINGTON, the Duke of Milton, regarded Alasdair with a closed expression. He had called at Hadley House before even taking his morning ride. He'd waited in the library for almost an hour.

Amusement shifted through Alasdair at the duke's disrespect. Perhaps he still saw Alasdair as unworthy of his daughter, for surely the man knew why he visited. When His Grace arrived, he had coolly taken in Alasdair reading one of his books by the fire, before offering him a drink, which Alasdair declined.

"Is my daughter without virtue?" His Grace snapped without preamble. He walked to his oak desk and sat. Though he reposed casually in the high wing back chair, Alasdair noted the tension in his shoulders.

Alasdair closed the copy of The Excursion he had been skimming. "I cannot remember Lady Willow not being virtuous," Alasdair responded blandly, resting the leather volume on the shelf.

Surprise flickered in the depth of the duke's eyes before he composed his face into a neutral mask. Did the man expect him to speak about the past? Alasdair had spent the night thinking of Willow, and for the first time in years, he had acknowledged how young she had been when she rejected him. How uncertain and fearful she must have felt. He'd admitted he should have fought for her more. He had experienced many 'should haves' for the long night, recognizing she wouldn't be blind today if not for her family's meddling and his insouciance.

Enough with what should have happened. He would direct his will and thoughts to now, to the future.

"I suppose you are here to ask for my daughter's hand in marriage?"

The duke's expression was serious, and the way he assessed Alasdair was almost discomfiting. Amusement curled through him, for he was not at all intimidated. He had nothing to prove to the man, and he only needed to be honest. "I am."

"Willow is no longer top shelf goods, and I will not provide a dowry for her. If the rumors are true, you need an heiress."

Anger knifed through Alasdair. *Top shelf goods?* "Willow is not a commodity to be referred to as 'goods.' I will not condone you disparaging her," he said icily.

Grudging respect flared in the duke's eyes, but the man remained seated and silent. Alasdair could not believe there had been a time he'd wanted to earn the duke's respect.

He stepped closer to his desk. "I am not requesting Willow's hand because I need her dowry, I love her, and I will do all in my power to convince her of my regard. I only sought to inform you of my intentions so you would not feel fear or uncertainty for her future. I never stopped loving her, and her blindness will not stop that. I do not see weakness. Only her resilience. I have known men in the war to kill themselves because of lost limbs and sight. Willow has adapted, she has lived, and she is still the same beautiful and passionate girl I knew."

The duke's eyes filled with speculation and something akin to hope.

Alasdair turned and walked toward the door before he said something further to create a deeper chasm between them.

"Westcliffe," Milton grumbled.

Alasdair faltered and spun around.

"You cannot give her the lifestyle she needs. You can hardly provide for your estates. How will you keep my daughter in the comfort she needs and deserves?"

He contemplated the duke, burying the anger at his words. Did he really believe this? Alasdair prowled to the duke's desk, cold purpose in his steps. He looked down on the man. "The life Willow deserves is one of freedom," he growled. "To be loved and trusted. Not to be caged by her family, who considers her an embarrassment."

The duke surged to his feet, rage lighting his eyes. "My daughter is not an embarrassment for us. You go too far, Westcliffe."

"Do I?" he snapped. "Has Willow left Hadley House in years? Has she been taken to the waters in Bath? The theater or opera in London? To Hyde Park for carriage rides? You clipped her wings when you should have done everything in your power, to ensure life for her goes on. You may not approve of me, but I promise I will cherish Willow."

A curious smile creased the duke's lips. "I do approve of you, Westcliffe."

Alasdair frowned.

"I know you to be an honorable man. Lord Liverpool and many others have spoken of your heroism in the war and how you fought for the lives of your men. I only needed to be sure you felt affection for my daughter, and you had not deliberately compromised her, thinking she possessed a dowry. I grant you permission to wed my daughter if she will have you."

Alasdair inclined his head. "Thank you." He turned to walk away, but Milton's next words froze him.

"If Willow accepts you I will provide her dowry."

Alasdair glanced back at the duke, taking his measure. "No."

Milton stiffened in surprise. "Do not be hasty, Westcliffe."

His hands on the doorknob, he spoke, "While it would be a relief, I will not have Willow believing I am marrying her for what she brings to my pocket. I already face the insurmountable odds of convincing her she will never be a burden to me. I have made several investments my banker and solicitors predict will be successful. If they are right, in a few months' time, Willow's dowry will be negligible."

"And if your predictions are wrong?" The duke snapped.

"I am the Marquess of Westcliffe. I have enough merchants and investors clamoring to work with me, for me to believe we'll survive even if my prophesy is incorrect. And if by some miracle it isn't...that is a risk I am willing to take," Alasdair said quietly, then walked through the door.

The only challenge he now faced was to convince Willow of his love.

CHAPTER 8

The sounds from the music room were hauntingly beautiful. Fingers rippled over the keyboard of the pianoforte with unsurpassed skill. He opened the door quietly, and from the way Willow's spine stiffened, Alasdair knew she realized he had entered the room.

After his meeting with the duke, he had sought her presence. Her grandmother had bidden him to wait in the drawing room, but he was pulled against his will toward the rousing sounds. Somehow, he had known it was Willow who played. She had been a good pianist when he knew her, but now she was brilliant.

The song ended. She gently closed the lid of the pianoforte and came to her feet gracefully. She looked ravishing with her hair piled high on her head, the loose tendril hiding the slight scar at her left temple. Willow was dressed in a high- waisted, bright yellow gown, her naked toes peeking from beneath the hem of her dress and petticoats. He smiled at that bit of unladylike appearance.

"You came."

He stepped further into the room. "Did you doubt I would?"

"No, I feared you would."

She walked toward him. "Let us retire to the drawing room. I am sure grandmother has ordered refreshments as she is no doubt in raptures over these dreadful developments."

He shifted to the side and watched with a feeling of admiration as she opened the door, walked precisely several paces down the foyer, and then turned right. There was no hesitation when her hand turned the knob, and he strolled behind her into the parlor.

She kept her back turned to him, and he could see the fine trembling in her frame. "Willow, I—"

She spun to face him. Her face was placid, her eyes wide. "Did you pursue me for my fortune?" she demanded, jutting her small chin high.

"Willow, I—"

She held up her hand and looked directly at him, her eyes as piercing as arrows. "It is a simple question, my lord. It can be answered with a yes or no."

His gut knotted. "No."

She closed her eyes and relief chased her features. He wanted to gather her in his arms and whisper reassurance. But what would he say? That he was never pursuing her? That he had been lost in her beauty, her wit, her resilience, and because of his lack of control, they had been caught in a compromising position?

"Are you impoverished?"

He would only give her truth. "Yes."

She backed away, the color draining from her face. Moving without any mishap, she walked to the sofa and sank into its depth. He was impressed when she reached for the tea trolley, her movements smooth and without hesitation, and poured them tea. Her finger remained gently curled over the tip of the cup as if to feel for the heat of the water as it rose. She prepared tea and cake as elegantly as any lady in her waiting room.

"Please join me for some refreshment," she said coolly and waved her hand to the sofa in front of her.

His admiration swelled. None of her earlier apprehension showed on her face. In fact, she looked like a woman on a mission.

He sat beside her and accepted her offering.

She slathered jam across a bun, placed the knife on the table, and then bit delicately into the treat. All so seamlessly. It made him realize how much she must have had to learn to do on her own.

She cocked her head to the side. "You are staring."

He arched a brow. "Is that so?"

"Hmmm," she murmured around another bite. "I can feel it. Your eyes have been spending an inordinate amount of time on my lips."

He chuckled, and she smiled. He enjoyed her teasing.

The laugh died out of her eyes. "While I would prefer to indulge in light conversation, I believe we have more serious matters to discuss." She curled her hands around her cup and shifted, staring at him. It was uncanny, her ability to look directly at the person without seeing them. "My father believes you have compromised me and demands we must wed."

"Yes." He wondered if now was the time to admit he had already met with the duke.

She nodded, then took a delicate sip of her tea. "I have tried to reassure him that nothing happened between us, only a chaste embrace, but it seems Quinton and grandmother have advised him otherwise." The becoming blush climbing her face caused a tender ache to unfurl within him.

Quinton should have waited for Alasdair to approach the duke. Damn his interfering friend. Alasdair could only imagine how she must have been embarrassed.

She cleared her throat delicately. "I think we must band together and refuse their edict. I am three and twenty and not a child. I already possess inferior circumstances, and I doubt rumors of our…our…kisses will ruin me."

"No," he said quietly. Alasdair observed the wild jerk of her pulse at the base of her neck. He wanted to lean in and trace its delicate flutter with the tip of his tongue and breathe in her scent.

She stiffened, a frown marring her features. "No? I beg you not to be intimidated by my father and be pressured into—"

Alasdair's low chuckle of amusement had her narrowing her eyes.

"No man can force me to move against my own heart and inclination," he drawled. "I made my offer to your father not because he or Quinton pressured me, but because I wanted to."

Her gasp echoed in the room.

"You want to marry me?" Disbelief was rife in her voice.

"Yes."

She lowered her cup to the center table and shifted even closer to him. "I am not sure you understand, Alasdair. I am without a dowry."

He wanted to gut her father for the embarrassment that coated her voice.

"You bring other treasures to me, Lady Willow, other than money or lands, treasures that are far more valuable."

Shaking her head in obvious confusion, she stood, then sat back down as if in a daze. She tilted her head toward him. "I know you are impoverished. My grandmother is never wrong about such matters. And the rumor is that you were interested in the ladies displayed on the marriage mart. Since grandmother told me of your financial straits, I realized you must be seeking an heiress to replenish your coffers and to help your family." She leaned forward and searched for his hands.

He met her halfway and pleasure coursed through him at their softness.

Her fingers tightened on his. "My father has promised to never provide a dowry for me to any man who is not wealthy in his own right. It is his way of protecting me from fortune hunting rakes. He will not bend his stance."

"I am aware of this."

Piercing green eyes ran over him as if she could see, and a curious smile slanted her lips. "Yet you wish to marry me?"

"Yes."

"But why? I offer you nothing."

The anger that surged through him was raw and wicked. He tugged her toward him, doing nothing to check his roughness. She tumbled into his chest with a soft *oomph*.

"Has it never occurred to you that I love you?"

Utter shock filled her eyes, then hope, then fear. "If you love me, I will never marry you." The conviction in her voice was palpable.

"Is that so," he murmured low and hard, his lips mere scant inches from her mouth.

Her cheeks darkened with anger. "Yes. I will not have your love wither to resentment, and I will not endure the heartache of loving someone, who will grow to hate me. I am willing to have an affair with you. Something so fleeting and beautiful that would burn away before we could form chains of hatred or love. I would marry you for any reason, but love. I would marry you for companionship, I would marry you so you could regain wealth and fortune if I had a dowry. I might even have married you if you had simply pitied me, but *never* because I love you or you love me," she sobbed. "And you need to make your estates solvent, how can I take that from you?"

"I am not the type of man to rely on finding an heiress alone to fill my coffers, Willow. I have been making investments, and they have been bearing fruits. I also informed your father of my intentions, and he offered your dowry," he said flatly.

Surprised chased her features then relief. "He did?"

"Yes."

A look of wonder dawned on her face. "Father would only do that if he believed you to care for me."

Alasdair drew her even closer. "I love you, Willow. I never stopped. You are strong and beautiful. More capable than anyone I know to be without sight. You still dream, and I want to help you fulfill them all."

She tried to pull from him, but he held her firm.

"Please do not tell me such sentiments," she cried.

Frustration curled through him. "Will you marry me?"

Her chest heaved. "No."

"Is your only objection because I love you?"

She lowered her gaze, gathering her composure before opening her beautiful eyes to him. "Yes. I will not endure your love turning to disdain," she whispered hoarsely.

He cupped her cheeks and dipped his head so his lips brushed against hers, infusing coldness in his tone. "Then I will never speak of love again for you understand nothing. But you will marry me, and we will exchange our wants and needs in our bed. I will take you riding, swimming, to country dances and lavish balls, and I will be your anchor when you falter…always." He pressed a hard kiss to her lips, stroking his tongue over her teeth, and with a forceful push sank into the depth of her sweetness.

He kissed her for unending seconds, devouring her hot honeyed taste, uncaring someone could enter the parlor at any moment. She responded with such eagerness, his cock surged to life with painful immediacy, and the emotions roiling in him begged for an outlet in the depth of her body. He pulled from her, breathing raggedly. "If you only want lust between us, you will be ready for me, either on your back or on your knees. However I crave, whenever I want to take you."

Her face colored at his crudeness, but he continued, "And you will give me an heir and your fidelity, your joy, and laughter, but not your love. Is such a proposition suitable for you, Lady Willow?"

She closed her eyes, reining in the wash of emotions that had chased her lovely features too quick for him to decipher. When she opened her eyes, the green orbs were composed. "Yes, such terms are acceptable to me."

He was torn between throttling her and kissing her senseless. But he was the bigger fool. Because he had long realized he would take her in any condition he could get.

"Then you best to prepare for a wedding, my lady."

Alasdair sealed his words with a kiss.

CHAPTER 9

It had been two weeks since Alasdair had proposed. And in that time, Willow's disquiet had only grown, but so had her joy. Everything she had ever desired was hers for the claiming, if she would only embrace all he promised. She had met with his mother, and while she had seemed stiff and formal, she had made some effort to bend the last few days. His sisters had been wonderful. They made every effort to converse and put her at ease when she dined at Westerham Park on the previous evening.

Willow's family was overjoyed, and her grandmother could not understand why she was not suffused with happiness. Alasdair, despite his cold words, was kind, charming, and attentive.

The door to the drawing room opened, and from the weight of the footsteps, she surmised it was the butler.

"My lady," Dawson murmured. "A note has arrived from Westerham Park."

Disappointment lodged in her gut. "What does it say?"

There was a rustle of sound, and then he spoke, "It says the marquess sends his apologies and asks to reschedule your ride out. He has been called away to London on an urgent matter."

"Thank you, Dawson."

She waited until the door closed quietly before wilting against the sofa. Instead of being disappointed, she could look at this as a reprieve. Alasdair had coaxed her into agreeing to attempt to mount a horse. They had made plans, and she had waited with such excitement to know he would share this with her.

She had dressed in her finest riding habit and had even donned the matching hat, perching it at a jaunty angle on her head. It was a pity he had been called away. She smiled knowing he would do his best to make it up.

The thought froze her, and her pulse jumped in her throat.

Willow stood and measured her steps to the window, pressing her palm against the surface, imagining she could see the grass and the rolling lawns of the estate. This had been the third time he had been called away. The third time he had cancelled one of their meetings in a matter of two weeks. He had always apologized and made up for it with long conversations, or a walk, or even the picnic they indulged in over the weekend.

She could envision what their future would be like. He was a marquess with untold responsibilities. He would be away a lot, and at times when she needed him, he would be absent. And he would feel guilt, apologize, and do his utmost best to make amends. And the cycle would continue until he grew to resent her.

A deep ache burgeoned inside her, and she closed her eyes against it. She loved him desperately. But how could she go ahead with the small intimate wedding they had planned tomorrow in the chapel at Hadley House? Alasdair had procured a special license, probably in the fear she would change her mind.

A heavy weight settled over her heart as fear slithered through her. The last thing she wanted to do was hurt him, but she could not decide which would ravage him more. Marrying him or not marrying him. She pushed the doubts from her mind. *Not today*. This morning should have been about relearning her beautiful horse, Daisy. Willow pressed her face against the glass, feeling the heat of the sun. How she wished she was brave enough to traverse the path to the stables alone. Grayson had not come home, and Quinton had left for Dorset early this morning. Her father was secreted in his office with the estate manager, and her mother would only bombard Willow with dire predictions of the risks of riding.

Without giving fear the time to take hold of her, she walked from the parlor measuring all of her steps until she exited the house. She gloried in the sun's warmth, the nip of the breeze as it glided over her skin. She turned left, then strolled toward the copse of trees, feeling the barks and memorizing where they had stood in relation to the stables. Willow walked for a few minutes, the roar of her heart a thunder in her ears, bracing herself to hear the panicked shrill of her name from her mother's lips or the cry of alarm from one of the servants. When no cry sounded, she pushed her misgivings aside and pressed on, only pausing to inhale deeply, trusting her senses to direct her. She stumbled several times, trying to remember the layout to the stables, but it was not long before she came upon it. The sounds of the soft neighs, the smell of hay, sweat, and leather greeted her. Pleasure and fear coursed through her. The need burned in her, a relentless ache to act without fear, to do something for herself without seeking help.

"My lady!?" A voice rife with alarm spoke. The head groom.

She shifted toward his voice. "Hello, Thompson. Is Daisy readied?"

The order to prepare her horse had been sent down earlier when it had been believed Alasdair would escort her.

After a beat of silence, he responded, "Yes, Lady Willow."

"Good," she said brusquely. "Take my hand and lead me to her."

He complied, no doubt shocked by her presence and orders.

"Here you go, my lady."

"Thank you, Mr. Thompson." She inhaled to steady her nerves. "Please remove the side saddle, and re-saddle her. I will be riding astride."

"Yes, my lady."

A few minutes later Thompson directed her to

Daisy. All anxiety faded once she heard the snicker of welcome from her beloved horse. A lump formed in her throat and tears spilled down her cheeks. "Oh, Daisy," Willow crooned, reaching up to hug her neck. "You haven't forgotten me, have you? Even after all these years."

A surge of intense love for her animal filled Willow. She had missed her so much. How could she have stayed away for so long? Daisy nuzzled her, and Willow laughed, suddenly feeling free.

She carefully glided around her horse, feeling for the mounting block.

"Let me help you, my lady," Thompson said softly.

Willow smiled, grateful he had not departed. With his assistance, she was now comfortably seated on top of her horse. *Oh.*

Anxiety curled through her, and she stilled. As if sensing her fear, Daisy shifted, a bit too suddenly for Willow. Her heart rate accelerated, and she gripped the reins tightly.

You are strong and beautiful.

The ghost of Alasdair's passionate assurance whispered through her. Willow swallowed. He saw her in such a different light. He thought her so capable, so bold and stalwart. Why did she not believe the same? The painful realization that she was limiting herself, in the same manner her over-protective family did, caused her to release a harsh breath. Willow had been the one to refuse to ride, though Quinton had offered to assist her with riding several times. She was the one who firmly believed Alasdair would see her as a burden. She hardly asked anyone to aid her at Hadley House, and the tasks the servants did for her, would have been the same if she hadn't been without sight.

A soft moan slipped from her. Could it really be true? She frantically thought back on her life. While she fought with her mother on many things, most of the time Willow stopped herself from doing things because of her own doubts.

No more. *Not if I am to be Alasdair's marchioness.* She would need to be even bolder and sure. She would host dinner parties, play with their babies.

Oh God, children. How would she care for them? Before she allowed any other fear to take root, she gently nudged Daisy's sides. Willow knew the minute they exited the stables. The heat of the sun washed over her skin, and she breathed in the crispness of the air into her lungs. She urged the horse into a slow canter, trusting Daisy to lead her safely.

Invariably, her thoughts turned to Alasdair. He had not professed any tender words since the day he had asked her to marry him, but the way he treated her did not disguise his feelings. Every thought, every gentle kiss, communicated his adoration.

Oh, Alasdair, I've missed you so much.

A rare feeling of pure, undiluted happiness poured through her, and she threw back her head, lifting her face to the sun. Willow relaxed, exhilaration twisting inside of her, and she laughed without any decorum.

"I will never tire of hearing you laugh," Alasdair's voice said quietly.

Willow gripped the reins on Daisy and spun her toward his voice.

"I did not hear you canter close."

"I am on foot," he murmured.

"Your horse?"

"Grazing a few feet away. I dismounted when I saw you and walked over. You are riding astride."

She could hear the pride in his voice, and her chest swelled. "When I had my accident, I was riding side saddle. I could not bring myself to sit on Daisy in such a manner earlier."

"I am pleased you went ahead without me. I was called away to London, but on my way out I realized I would much rather be here with you. I sent a letter ahead with my solicitors."

Emotions tightened her throat. He didn't question where she found the courage. He simply accepted she had always been capable. Why would she think such a man would ever find her to be burdensome?

"It will indeed be glorious to be the lady of Westerham Park," she offered in the companionable silence.

Firm hands pressed against her legs. She did not startle. She had smelled his alluring scent drifting closer. He gripped her hips and Willow relinquished the reins. She dismounted, clasping his shoulders, savoring the press of his body against her. The softest kiss brushed against her lips and sweet desire built.

He ended their too short embrace. He brushed his fingers gently over the points of her knuckles. "Let us stroll together, then we will eat. I still brought along the basket my cook prepared."

She placed her hand on his arms and moved with him, a delighted feeling of contentment suffusing her veins. "How did you come to be the marquess?"

She listened to the soft cadence of his voice, the

gentle dips as he told the story of his father and brothers. She heard the pain of loss in his voice, but also the acceptance. They came to a stop, and he leaned against a tree, drawing her into the comforting circle of his arms. They conversed at length, and Willow reveled in the moment and did her best to ignore the edge of doubts that still lingered.

CHAPTER 10

E veryone was gathered in the ancient chapel of Hadley House. Willow had wanted to pick flowers that morning in the gardens, but then the unexpected rain had fallen. Dressed in a simple but exquisite soft yellow gown, flowers decorating her hair, and a bouquet of rosebuds gripped tightly in her hand, her eyes were wide with apprehension, but she had never looked more beautiful.

After their walk and long talk the day before, Alasdair had not expected to see such a show of anxiety from her. But he understood this was a big step for her, and he was glad to note she had stopped speaking of her belief she was a burden. Instead, she had been avidly seeking his kisses, and the long talks and strolls they indulged in.

He squeezed her fingers in reassurance, and she favored him with a wobbly smile.

The Vicar started the ceremony. "Dearly beloved, we are gathered together here in the sight of God, and in the face of this congregation, to join together this Man and this Woman in holy Matrimony; which is an honourable estate, instituted of God in the time of man's innocency."

Alasdair listened to the Vicar's words his eyes never leaving Willow's face. She did not seem to be listening to the vicar or to him.

A few minutes later the Vicar turned to Alasdair. "Lord Alasdair Hugh Morley, Marquess of Westcliffe, wilt thou have this woman to thy wedded Wife, to live together after God's ordinance in the holy estate of Matrimony? Wilt thou love her, comfort her, honor, and keep her in sickness and in health; and, forsaking all other, keep thee only unto her, so long as ye both shall live?"

"I will," he vowed.

The Vicar shifted to Willow.

"Lady Willow Rosalind Arlington wilt thou have this man to thy wedded Husband, to live together after God's ordinance in the holy estate of Matrimony? Wilt thou obey him, and serve him, love, honor, and keep him in sickness and in health;

and, forsaking all other, keep thee only unto him, so long as ye both shall live?"

Her throat convulsed. "I…I…"

Tears pooled behind her lids and tension twisted through Alasdair. The patter of rain seemed to echo in the silence. No one spoke or moved. The Vicar cleared his throat and looked from her to Alasdair with a frown on his face.

"Willow?" Alasdair asked softly.

Her fingers trembled in his. His unease sharpened.

"I am so sorry." Her voice was hoarse with unshed tears.

His world narrowed to her face, taking in the grief and doubt in her eyes. "Please don't," he whispered, uncaring that everyone could hear him. "We will be fine, Willow. I love you."

Something in him broke when she lowered her hands and dropped the rosebuds.

He had lost her.

❦

SHE RAN.

"Willow!"

The harsh sound of her mother's voice rang

out, blending with the gentler tones of her father to let her go. But she did not hesitate. She burst through the doors of the chapel as if the devil were on her heels. Her mind drew maps of the house as she moved with more speed than she thought possible.

Please don't.

The quiet plea had been evident in Alasdair's voice. The bleakness. He sounded as if she had shredded something in him. The doubts almost drowned her. She had once again rejected him. He would hate her now. A harsh sob clawed from her throat as she stumbled up the stairs. She needed her room, her sanctuary, to still the mess of emotions suffocating her.

She couldn't do it. But how could she live without him? The pain of loss sliced through her. "Oh God, please let this pain stop," Willow moaned as she reached the landing. She turned right and tried to walk with measured steps, her fingers gliding against the wall's surface. She came to the fourth door and felt for the knob. She pushed inside, moving too fast and tripped.

She cried out as she fell forward. Unable to check her momentum, she braced for the impact that never came. Gentle hands caught her.

She froze. He had followed her? She had not smelled or heard him. Relief crashed into her. He was there. "Alasdair." There was nothing calm about the way his name burst from her lips along with the sob. It was raw and ugly, and she did not care.

"Easy," he reassured. "I have you."

I will be your anchor when you falter…always.

Her chest constricted, and it seemed impossible to draw air. "I hurt you, again." She pressed a fist to her mouth as he drew her to him, leaning her against his chest. His heat was a comfort and a temptation. "Forgive me, I never wanted to bring you pain ever again."

His heat shifted slightly, and the door to her chamber closed. The snick of the lock as he thumbed it had her swallowing. "My parents will come."

"No one would dare come up here. They understand I am trying to persuade you to be my wife. That I am trying to convince you of the depth and breadth of my love. The hounds of hell will not part me from you now, Willow. They saw that. I am the only one that followed you. The others have dispersed to the lawns."

She nodded, her throat tightening. There was

no anger in his voice, no pain, only patience, and understanding. This man loved her. Treasured her. He had been willing to marry her even without a dowry. Oh God, what had she done? "And the vicar?"

"I told the family and the vicar they can leave if we do not return. If we do not marry today I will not panic," he said softly.

She waited for Alasdair to say more, to berate her, and nothing. The tension eased from her, and she relaxed into him. "You are not angry," she observed fighting to control the pounding of her heart.

"No."

"You are disappointed."

"No."

"You are hurt."

He pushed her forward, walking deeper into her room.

"I feel only relief that I am holding you. All else faded the moment I touched you," he confessed, raw emotions evident in his voice.

"Hold me, Alasdair, and do not let me go, ever."

He drew her into his arms and hugged her tightly.

"Marry me, and you will never regret loving me," Alasdair promised fiercely.

Her mind swirled, and her body came alive at the promise in his tone. If she didn't trust him, the clawing empty ache that had been living inside her since the moment she told him she didn't love him years ago would never be filled. And she loved him so much, she wept from the intensity. She had never stopped either, and since he came back, the possibilities of true happiness had been hovering, and she was tired of doubts belittling her joy. Only a fool would think the future was absolutely certain. And Willow was no fool. She wiggled in his arms, and he gave her enough space so she could tug his lips to her. "I want you, now and always—"

Her words were smothered as he seized her lips in a powerful kiss. Desire shot through her. His tongue stroked into her mouth with exquisite thoroughness, and any resistance she possessed caught fire and burned to ashes in mere seconds. He smelled lush and rich—evocative. He tasted even better. Alasdair pressed kisses over the arc of her throat, muttering sweet nonsense as he stormed all her defenses with bliss.

"I need you, Alasdair, love me," she urged huskily.

He pulled from her. Sounds shifted in the room, and she inhaled sharply as she interpreted the sound of his shirt being drawn over his head and tossed away, followed by the soft purr of his breeches sliding off his skin. She waited, laden heat surging through her limbs. He pressed her body to his, and she jolted at the contact.

He was naked.

He undressed her in silence. Slowly unfastening the tiny buttons that adorned the back of the stiff satin of her dress, she listened to it as it swished to the carpet. He untied her lace festooned petticoats, and they joined her dress around her feet. His fingers moved to unlace her stays and swiftly they too slithered to the ground.

He turned her to him, and her heart clenched at the kiss he pressed against her forehead.

She stroked her hands over well-defined muscles, enjoying the heat and power of his body. Her fingers trailed over his abdomen down to his thighs and brushed against the heated length of him. She gasped at the silky feel. Her fingertips glided over his shaft, and a muttered curse slipped from him. He was long and thick, and she could feel the pulsing need within him. Willow had seen the male form presented in sculptures and paintings.

And had been avidly curious about those parts that were so different from hers. The reality far exceeded everything she could have imagined. She gripped him tightly, her fingers barely closing around his length. As a whole he was magnificent. And she desperately wanted him. He buried his face in her neck, inhaled deeply, then gently stroked the tip of his finger over her back.

"Don't ever doubt me, Willow. Don't walk away from me, from this, from us," he said, his voice now roughened.

His words splintered the dam of doubt she had been clinging onto. "Yes," she whispered. "Never again. Whenever I falter, I will *always* trust you."

That was all it took.

He yanked her hard against his chest and claimed her lips. Devoured her. He trailed kisses against her neck and down to her breasts, which were heavy with arousal. She bucked as he flicked his tongue over her throbbing nipple. As if impatient, he swung her into his arms and carried her to the bed in the center of the room. He laid her down and kept trailing kisses over her body without breaking his tender assault. He slid his tongue down to her stomach, licking her navel, and then even lower to her most intimate valley.

Willow's breathing fractured as confusion and lust hazed her mind. He wouldn't. He did. She arched her hips, lost in the bliss twisting through her veins. He licked and nibbled at her wet flesh, drawing moans and whimpers from her lips.

Her body was on fire with sensations.

She lowered her hand, feeling and encountering his head. It seemed the most natural thing in the world to grip the strands of his curly hair as she arched even more onto his tormenting tongue. She was rewarded with waves of ecstasy splintering through her body. He did not stop his sensual assault, now combining fingers with his tongue. He slipped one, two, and then three fingers inside of her slickness.

"Alasdair," she gasped.

The sharp bite of pain had a sob clawing from her throat. Then the sweetest of pleasure rushed through her veins. She lost awareness of everything, but the feel of his fingers deep inside of her.

He climbed over her, all power and grace. The heat of his body, the strength of him, caged her, protected even as it intimidated. He was pure hardness where she was voluptuously soft. He tilted her hips and pressed against her wet aching entrance, and then he plunged deep. Willow gasped at the shock of his entry, tightening her grip on his sweat slicked shoulders.

Alasdair held himself still, kissing her until she squirmed, desperate for him to move and end the pressure low in her stomach. But a greater need to bare her soul to him rose in her.

"I should never have run from your love, your passion. I feel safe with you," she confessed. "I feel loved and protected. I feel like me. Like nothing has changed, and I can be who I am, without being pitied and doubted. I worried my disability would wear on you and eventually turn you to disdain. But I see now that it is not possible. Because you love me with all your being. The adoration I feel in your touch can never fade. And I love you with all of me, Alasdair."

He trembled in reaction to her declaration, dropping his forehead to hers.

She coasted her hands over his back, and curved her hands possessively over his buttocks, pressed her heels into the bed and arched up to him. It was all the encouragement he needed.

Sweet heavens. The pull of his flesh as he withdrew and then sank into her was glorious. Pleasure cascaded through her and she moaned into his kiss, loving the strength he took her with.

She did not feel fragile, but like a woman, his woman. She gloried in the feel of his powerful body surging inside of her. The sweetest erotic pain blended with the pleasure of each deep thrust, but she never wanted him to stop.

She never wanted this interlude to end.

She loved him.

Alasdair kept his thrusts slow and deep, delighting in the way Willow clung to him, and the sweet moans spilling from her throat. Passionately, she yielded to him, and he took it all. It was a feast of the senses as they licked and explored each other. Every touch was an imprint, a brand across his soul. Every sob of pleasure that slipped from her chained him deeper into need. He had to give her everything.

Her delicate fingers skimmed across his brow.

"I desire to be your wife, Alasdair."

He stilled his thrusting and peered down at her. Joy, wonder, and lust suffused her face. She lifted her mouth to his, and he succumbed to the need burning inside of him. She did not wrest his control from him, he willingly surrendered it at her declaration, trusting her to meet his passion.

He nudged her legs open wider, pushing her knees back toward her shoulder and sank into her with stunning strength. Her cries wrapped around him, soothing and encouraging. She gripped him with sublime tightness, a litany of love spilling from her lips as he rode her with deep hard thrusts. She clawed at his back, undulated her hips against his strokes, taking him, chaining him to the desire that flowed between them.

He swallowed her moans, smothering his shout of satisfaction, as she rippled over his cock tighter than anything he had ever felt, drawing his release from him. He tumbled with her into more than pleasure.

He dived into love and the promise of happiness with her.

EPILOGUE

Fifteen months later

"Our daughter has your features. Beautiful dark hair, the greenest of eyes and the palest of skin. I can see I will have gray hair before my time."

His sweet wife chuckled, delight chasing her features.

"And our son?" she asked, glancing toward his voice.

Alasdair gaze shifted to the babe cradled on Willow's left side. "A perfect little man, but he has more of my features."

She had only given birth a few hours ago, but

she glowed with love and excitement instead of exhaustion.

"Aren't they perfect?" she crooned, dipping to inhale their scent before placing gentle kisses unerringly on the tops of their heads.

The past year had been filled with passion and adventure. Willow still played the pianoforte every morning but also added horse riding as a part of her routine. At first, she had been hesitant in how far she rode Daisy, and Alasdair had been with her every step of the way, guiding and helping her. Within weeks, she had been galloping across the plains of the estate, trusting him and her horse, recalling her former skill as an expert horsewoman. He had not been surprised when only after six months of marriage she had become with child. He made love to her every night and at least twice in the day.

She ran Westerham Park better than even his mother could have imagined. They had become fast friends, and Willow had implored her to live with them at the estate and not retire to the dowager house. His mother had joyfully complied, and he had watched the growth of the relationships between his marchioness and his mother and sisters with avid fascination. At first, Willow had been hesitant then she had blossomed. She charmed them with her strength and her vivacity for life. He had witnessed his mother's wariness swell into admiration, then respect, and then love.

The Duke of Milton had insisted on settling Willow's dowry on them, and since Alasdair had no longer needed her money since his investments had returned tenfold, he had placed the dowry into a trust for his wife and children. Her father had shaken his hand and gruffly told Alasdair he had waited a damn long time to return for her.

"We did well, didn't we," Willow murmured in awe, when their son stirred and let out a small cry.

Alasdair climbed onto the bed beside her, gently gathering her close, careful not to disturb the twins' comfort as they lay upon her chest suckling. His mother had thought it unfashionable Willow refused to employ a wet nurse, but she had insisted on providing for her babes herself, wanting to be as close to them as possible.

"We did brilliantly my love," he whispered, dipping his head to kiss her lips softly. He breathed in deep, loving her fresh, clean scent that was peppered with the right hint of lavender. Warmth poured through him as her lips curved into a smile and unguarded happiness filled her eyes.

"I love you, Lady Westcliffe," he whispered.

"And I love you, Alasdair, I think nearly as much as I love our twins."

"I will have to lock you in the clock tower like a jealous ogre until you promise you love me most," he teased.

"It is far too noisy to sleep in the clock tower."

"I doubt if it is noisier than the twins in full cry," he leaned over and kissed her even deeper, and his son and heir let out an annoyed scream in complaint. They laughed together as Willow replaced her son and he went back to contented guzzling.

Alasdair thought life was as perfect as his marchioness…

THANK you for reading **The Marquess and I**!

I hope you enjoyed the journey to happy ever after for Alasdair and Willow. **REVIEWS ARE GOLD TO AUTHORS,** for they are a very important part of reaching readers, and I do hope you will consider leaving an honest review on Amazon adding to my rainbow. It does not have to be lengthy, a simple sentence or two will do. Just know that I will appreciate your efforts sincerely.

CONTINUE READING FOR A SNEAK PEEK INTO THE NEXT BOOK OF THE SERIES

THE DUKE AND I

Forever Yours Series Book 2
Excerpt

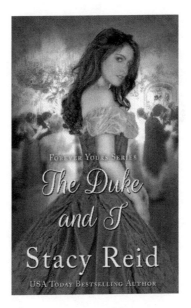

Grab a Copy Today

FAR BE it for a lady to desire, hatch, and execute a daring seduction of a notorious duke at a masquerade ball. But Miss Emmaline Fitzgerald, a wallflower with no decent prospects, was on such a path, and her quarry was her brother's best friend, Elliot Winthrop, the Duke of Ashbrook.

One moment of sin, stolen pleasure, and irresistible passion, that was all it was supposed to be....

Little did Emma realized everything about her was imprinted in Elliot's heart and mind, and her scandalous ruse was about to change and challenge everything she thought she knew about herself and the devilish duke.

CHAPTER ONE

Bellview Manor, Chiswick, England 1818

IT WAS the unhappiest news imaginable.

Elliot George Ashbrook, the ninth Duke of Hartford was about to marry or make an announcement of some sorts that he was ready to settle down. All the marriage-minded mammas of the season would be deliriously overjoyed, and then the hunt for who would secure such a worthy and estimable match would commence with genteel vigor. Society would be atwitter for months, and all the newspapers would write about this unprecedented move by the duke. For so long society had declared him a scoundrel, a rake of the first order.

Miss Emma Amelia Fitzgerald pressed a fist to her chest as if that would stop the sudden ache that settled heavily in her heart. Elliot was to find a bride. The hand that had been poised to knock on the door to the study lowered. She had to gather her composure before facing her brother and his guest. It would not do for the duke to see the sheen of tears in her eyes or the pain that must be evident on a face that many had declared to be expressive. After all, it had been she who had rejected his offers of marriage several years ago. Although she did not regret her decision and despite her current situation a small part of her dearly wished he would renew his addresses. He had not asked her again, and her pride, doubts, and fear had prevented her from approaching him. Years had passed, eight to be exact. And she had realized he must have accepted she was impaired and unmarriageable.

"I did not realize you'd hoped to settle down," her brother, Anthony Fitzgerald, said. "I thought you cherished your liberty greatly."

"I've decided it's time," Elliot drawled. "I am nine and twenty and not getting any younger. I'll signal my intention by attending Lady Wiles' ball in two weeks' time."

Elliot hadn't visited Bellview Manor in almost six months. The duke's voice was richer and deeper, more confident than she remembered.

A rough sound of disbelief issued from her bother. "You are entirely serious. I cannot credit it. You have been a right rogue these last seasons. The polite world will be shocked and delighted. Do you have someone in mind?"

There was a contemplative pause.

"Perhaps Lady Andrea Sutton. She appears to be the most accomplished debutante of this season. I had the pleasure to dance with her last season and found her to be quite good-natured and intelligent."

"Not to mention stunningly beautiful and perfect."

Perfect. Everything Emma was not after the terrible carriage accident. The one her brother still blamed himself for because it had limited her prospects for marriage and a future. And because it had taken the man she loved…still loved if she was honest, the duke himself. Except when she had fallen hopelessly in love with him, he hadn't been a duke. They had been friends, neighbors, and everything then had seemed so simple, her place in the world defined and understood. Her expectations of marrying Elliot then and starting a family had been real and attainable, but in an instant, it had all been ripped away to be replaced by broken limbs and a hopeless heart. Her only solace was a change of scene, which she would achieve by travelling to Boston.

"Perfection is not a criterion of mine, but it does not hurt that she presents a very pretty picture."

There was a slight easing in her heart at that declaration.

Anthony said something she could not decipher, and she was so tempted to press her ear to the wooden panel. It was unforgivably rude to eavesdrop, but she consoled her conscience by recalling her need to gather composure before facing her brother and the duke. It pained her to admit even for a second she wanted to retreat to the music room and resume playing the pianoforte. But she had never been a coward, and she would not start on this auspicious visit.

"Will I see you next week at Lady Waverly's house party?" Elliot asked.

Emma stiffened. That scandalous house party had been on the lips of many in society for weeks. The countess's yearly house party and her masquerade ball were notorious and only the rogues, the scoundrels, and the most scandalous women of the season attended. Though from what Emma had gathered from the scandal sheets over the years, genteel ladies had donned masks and wigs to attend and had fallen to ruin.

"You know you won't find a wife there."

There was a low chuckle of masculine amusement. "That will be for pleasure," the duke drawled. "The countess's parties are always so amusing. I plan to indulge with a willing lady or two before I make my intentions to find a bride this season known."

A willing lady or two? The duke was indeed the worst sort of scoundrel. And her older brother's best friend. And the man she still loved with her entire soul.

"Why bother? You left the last masquerade

without a lady on your arm, and the previous two before that if I recall correctly."

An annoyed grunt came from the duke. "There should be enough daring beauties to satisfy my discriminating tastes there this year."

The sound of glasses clinking echoed.

"How is Emma?"

Her heart shivered at the mention of her name.

"Still refusing to marry and insisting on taking an extended trip to America. I cannot imagine why she would want to visit that wild place."

The silence that lingered prompted her to lift her fist to knock on the door once more, but instead, she ran her hand over her light-blue, muslin, day dress smoothing non-existing wrinkles. She then took a deep breath and closed her eyes running a quick mental check over herself. Emma patted her stunning, bright red hair ensuring the artful chignon her maid had arranged had no loose wisps. She was in a presentable state to face him. She raised her hand to knock once again and paused as the duke's voice filtered through the door once more.

"You do not wish for her to leave?"

Was it her fanciful imagination that Elliot's voice sounded out of sorts?

"No, we all want to see her content in her own home with a husband and children. Father and I have discussed it. He will forbid her travelling."

Outrage snapped through Emma. Why did papa insist on ruling her life even though she was of age? It was not as if she were travelling to people who she knew nothing about. Her older sister, Elizabeth, had married an American business magnate and was blissfully settled in Boston. She had invited Emma over to meet their society, confident she would find some measure of happiness there. Though Emma doubted any such happiness would exist for her, she was thrilled with the notion of leaving England's shores for an extended period. Her family had not been happy to receive her news.

"What are her chances of making a respectable alliance?"

"At five and twenty? Little to none. There is something else," he muttered, sounding a trifle apprehensive. "Lord Coventry has declared his wish to marry her, and our father has agreed. Emma has no notion of the alliance."

Shock froze her. She had not heard of this outrage.

"Coventry! The man can't be a day under

sixty." There was a thoughtful pause, and then the duke said, "Will she have him? You know she is very decided with her opinions."

"Deuced stubborn and fanciful, that's what she is."

"Still, the old earl cannot be acceptable. Emma will not be happy with your decision. Hell, I'm not happy with it," Elliot said gruffly, a vein of surprise in his tone.

"The task of arranging her a proper match is harder than I'd imagined. She does not make it easy."

"You know it to be more. She is still hurt from…"

Her stomach knotted at the mention of her accident. Unable to tolerate the tone their discussion was taking, she knocked firmly and entered, moving carefully.

"Anthony dearest, I—" She paused, quite dramatically. "Your grace, I wasn't aware you had called."

Emma shifted to face him fully. She wasn't prepared for the impact of sensations upon seeing him. Pleasure and nerves. The duke's tall frame was one of powerful, lithe elegance. His dark hair was perfectly groomed, and his beautiful golden eyes ensnared her. His dark lashes were velveted soft and so long, she noticed as he bowed over her hand. His hands were strong and firm, and she was relieved when he let go of her fingers because the fleeting touch sent a thrill up her spine. Elliot was held to be driven and intense, reputed to be brilliant in business, a thing which had shocked society for a duke had no reason to be doing anything but being a duke. Even after eight years of mingling with the *ton*, Elliot was an enigma to both the press and society and unfortunately, a bit reserved and cold. Especially towards her.

Still, a frightening surge of longing and an ache travelled through her heart. He had only to be in the same room, and the response came unbidden.

The arrogant lift of his eyebrow and the amused slant of his lips said he knew her to be lying. Then his eyes dropped to her walking stick, and her gut tightened. It was always the first place someone looked, at the stick, and then her limp, and then pity would cross their features, and their voices would soften dramatically as if she were addled and they needed to speak with care.

How wretched it made her feel. Only a few people conversed with her without any undertones of pity and speculation.

"How wonderful to see you again, Miss Fitzgerald."

How formal he was, as if there hadn't been a time they had swum together in the pond, as if he hadn't taught her to fish, and as if he hadn't kissed her once, and stolen her heart away.

Relief filled her that he sounded normal, and his eyes had returned to her face. Not that he had ever treated her as an invalid, but it had been a while since they had cause to be in each other's company. She had never been able to predict his responses to her entirely. "It has been six months," she said pertly, wincing at the soft reprimand in her voice.

His expression was faintly amused. "Has it?"

His eyes were the deep gold of a lion, so stunning and unique. There had always been a profound stillness in his gaze, one that she felt she couldn't touch or understand, one that seemed to hold a thousand secrets. She'd always thought she was fanciful, unsure if the sensation of danger was real or an illusion. They stared at each other until her brother cleared his throat. She flushed and glanced away.

"Forgive me for interrupting you, Anthony. I've

invited Vicar Marbury, his wife, and delightful daughter to dinner. I trust this is acceptable?"

Her brother scowled. "Do I have to be there? You know how Miss Marbury…she is too attentive."

Emma thought it served him right for being so odious in encouraging papa once again to select a husband for her, despite her stated wish not to marry. "I'm sure she'll be charming company." Emma faced Elliot. "Should I inform the housekeeper to set a place for you as well, Your Grace?"

"Regretfully I must decline. I have a previous engagement I cannot avoid."

"Of course." She gave him a small smile that felt too tight. "If I could speak with Anthony for a few minutes in privacy?"

"I was just about to take my leave," Elliot said smoothly. He dipped his head in a short bow and made his exit.

The door closed firmly on the duke's departure, and she made her way to the blue damask sofa and lowered herself, carefully arranging her walking stick to the side. She considered her brother for a few moments. It was mortifying to admit she had been eavesdropping, but she could not allow him and papa to decide her life as if she had no thoughts or hopes of her own.

Her family did nothing that did not administer to their own comfort, and it was evident they wanted her off their hands. A peculiar grief darted through her. "I've tried not to be a burden despite my limitations."

He shot her a reproving glance. "You are my sister, and I love you, Emma. You have never been a burden and never will be. You speak nonsense."

"Then why did you not tell me Papa was speaking with Lord Coventry about marriage? Is that not for your own comfort? For surely you could not believe I have any affection for the earl."

He raked his fingers through his hair. "I want what is best for you," he said with soft intensity. "Our family wants what is best for you."

"That would be allowing me to live my life however it makes me happy, Anthony."

"Do you not want a family, Emma? Children of your own."

A surge of longing darted through her heart, and a lump grew in her throat. She wanted a family, love, comfort, security, and happiness. She acknowledged the argument that she was like other women in wanting those things, but there was also an untapped desire that had brewed in her soul over the years. It had grown as she had come to terms with the fact that she was maimed. That part of her desired adventure, something different from the terrible predictability that was her life. Quite often the two needs mashed together painfully inside, disturbing any contentment she found with her current situation. Marrying Coventry when she did not love him, and when she would be the object of his pity and derision was not the sort of life she wanted. "Not with Coventry."

Her brother's brows came together in a considering frown. "He is only two and forty. He likes you despite...despite." He broke off with a frustrated growl.

Emma stood. "Despite my scars which he has not seen? Despite my limping? Despite that, on the days when the cramps are terrible, I use a wheelchair? Despite the fact I may truly never be able to have children? Did you or papa inform him of all the facts when he made his offer?"

His expression hardened. "He will call upon you tomorrow. I expect you to be courteous and give him a fair chance."

"I cannot promise to be available."

"You are unreasonable."

"I am not," she said firmly. "The last suitor you and papa pushed in my path informed me in no uncertain terms when we wed, I would remain in the country and never venture into society. I hadn't even accepted his offer, and he was ashamed of my situation. I cannot bear being trapped with anyone who would make me feel inferior and an object to be pitied. Can you assure me Lord Coventry would be different?"

Before her brother could reply, the door opened and in sailed their aunt Beatrice, who despite her short and plump stature, looked very elegant in a dark green riding habit, and matching hat with a decorative dyed feather. Bright blue eyes scanned the drawing room. "How delightful that you are both here! I've just arrived from Bath where I left your father and mother taking the waters. I've heard the wonderful news that Lord Coventry will be courting you. I thought you would need my guidance, my dear."

Exasperation rushed through Emma. "Not you too, Aunt Beatrice."

Her aunt shot her a bird-like look of inquiry. "But this is great news is it not?"

"No, it is not, I have no wish to be courted by Lord Coventry."

"But he is an earl!"

"My goodness, I'm a trifle tired. I am sure Anthony will explain." She ambled over to him and pressed a kiss to his cheek. "Thank you for caring, brother, but I do not need you to direct my life, just to love and support me."

Anthony scowled. "Emma—"

She walked away from his absurd orders, and her aunt's query of 'upon my word, have her senses departed her?' Emma moved out into the hallway, closing the door softly on her exit. Her family wanted her to be happy. She supposed one had to make allowances for that. But she would not let them dictate her life when she was of age, and had an inheritance of five thousand pounds and could manage her affairs herself. They evidently thought her an invalid and were willing to foist her onto the first man who showed some interest in her.

Except for Elliot…

Her throat tightened with remembered pain and happiness.

The acquaintance between herself and the duke had been longstanding, except he hadn't been the powerful and arrogant duke of Hartford then, merely the charming, good-natured, and ambitious Mr. Elliot Winthrop.

She was the second daughter of a gentleman, the viscount Sherwood, and Elliot was the son of the local doctor. He'd always treated her with kindness and pleasant sweetness, never objecting as her brother had done when she insisted on riding astride in breeches with them across the fens or swimming in the lake in her chemisette, their laughter ringing across windswept grasslands. He hadn't thought her improper or ill-bred as her brother had often lamented, but had merely encouraged her to be daring and true to her own nature.

She had been fifteen at the time, to Elliot's nineteen, and had been quite desperately in love with her brother's friend. She had known without a doubt he was the man she would marry and had believed he felt a similar attachment.

Life had seemed happy, then the curricle race had happened, and everything had been unbearable for months. When Elliot had asked her to marry him while she lay hurt in bed, with pity in his eyes, she had said no for she had loved him too much to saddle him with a broken wife. He'd asked again, and she'd said no. She'd cared deeply that the two doctors her papa had consulted with, had declared the possibility of her never walking or having children because of her injuries. Her family had objected most passionately for he'd had no connections and wealth and had aspired to visit Edinburgh to study and become a doctor like his father. That aspect hadn't mattered to Emma though. He had renewed his offer several times over the next few months, and she had refused until he had stopped asking.

Then a few months later what had seemed like an army of solicitors and the Duchess of Hartford had tracked him down to Devon. Her Elliot had been the next in line for a dukedom.

'Don't forget me,' she'd whispered fervently when he had been collected by the duchess whom Emma had dubbed the dragon.

'Will you…remember me?' she had asked with such aching sadness.

He'd given her a brief, wordless nod. Instead of walking away he stood for a timeless moment. "Wait for me, promise."

Her heart had soared with gladness. "I will," she'd replied, though knowing in her heart once he glimpsed the world before him, he wouldn't care to remember the broken daughter of an impoverished viscount. Eager to keep her promise to Elliot, she had written to him often, but he had been an indifferent correspondent, only replying to a few of the dozens of letters she had posted to him.

Of course, he had become imminently suitable to her family after it was confirmed he was the next duke of Hartford.

And now he was about to announce to polite society his intention to take a wife.

Emma made her way down the quiet hall at an unhurried pace. She paused at the bottom of the stairs, resting her head briefly on the banister. Why did her heart feel so laden with grief and regrets? It had taken years before she had been able to imagine a future without Elliot. She'd already made plans for her life, and she would see them through. If only before she left for America, she could dance with him, just once, or perhaps even kiss him, and perhaps just a bit more.

The thought arrested her.

What if…?

And suddenly she knew. Before she departed the shores of England, before she lost him forever, she would have one moment of sin, of stolen pleasure, and irresistible passion.

Instead of ascending the stairs, she made her way to the music room where her younger sister

Maryann played the pianoforte. Emma entered, and her sister glanced up.

"Oh dear, you have *that* rebellious look in your eyes."

"I need your help, and I only have a week to prepare."

"Of course, whatever you need," she said with all the loyalty of a sister who loved her dearly.

She would attend Lady Waverly's house party, or better, the masquerade ball customarily held at its conclusion. "We will have to be *very* discreet."

Maryann's eyes widened, and one of her hand fluttered to her chest. "Oh, dear."

Emma would avail herself of its advantages, namely pursuing a sensual encounter with the duke of Hartford. The very idea was positively indecent, shocking, and scandalous, but there was a chance to experience something that she'd always wanted.

Emma could only hope afterward she would not be left in ruined disgrace.

WANT TO KNOW WHAT HAPPENS NEXT?

CONTINUE READING...

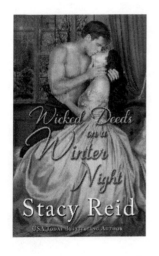

Happy reading!
Stacy Reid

ACKNOWLEDGMENTS

I thank God every day for my family, friends, and my writing. A special thank you to my husband. I love you so hard! Without your encouragement and steadfast support I would not be living my dream of being an author. You encourage me to dream and are always steadfast in your wonderful support. You read all my drafts, offer such amazing insight and encouragement. Thank you for designing my fabulous cover! Thank you for reminding me I am a warrior when I wanted to give up on so many things.

Thank you, Giselle Marks for being so wonderful and supportive always. You are a great critique partner and friend. Readers, thank you for giving me a chance and reading my book! I hope you enjoyed and would consider leaving a review. Thank you!

ABOUT STACY

USA Today Bestselling author Stacy Reid writes sensual Historical and Paranormal Romances and is the published author of over twenty books. Her debut novella The Duke's Shotgun Wedding was a 2015 HOLT Award of Merit recipient in the Romance Novella category, and her bestselling Wedded by Scandal series is recommended as Top picks at Night Owl Reviews, Fresh Fiction Reviews, and The Romance Reviews.

Stacy lives a lot in the worlds she creates and actively speaks to her characters (aloud). She has a warrior way "Never give up on dreams!" When she's not writing, Stacy spends a copious amount of time binge-watching series like The Walking Dead, Altered Carbon, Rise of the Phoenixes, Ten Miles of Peach Blosson, and playing video games with her love. She also has a weakness for ice cream and will have it as her main course.

Stacy is represented by Jill Marsal at Marsal Lyon Literary Agency.

She is always happy to hear from readers and would love to connect with you via my Website, Facebook, and Twitter. To be the first to hear about her new releases, get cover reveals, and excerpts you won't find anywhere else, sign up for her newsletter, or join her over at Historical Hellions, her fan group!